SEWN AT THE CRIME

STITCHES IN CRIME - BOOK 6

ACF BOOKENS

1

I've always known the building was Anderson School. Dad had told me that much. But in the way of things that are always there, I hadn't really thought to ask many questions. I knew what I knew, and I thought that was all there was to know — until I got older and really learned about Jim Crow and segregation, until I realized that some of my friends wouldn't have been allowed to go to the same school as me. It took me far too long to learn that.

But when I did, Anderson suddenly became more than just an old, graying building off the road near Dad's house. Then, it became a place full of history and stories, a place where people I loved had gotten their education, same as I had over at Woodbright in town. If I could still remember the smell of the mimeograph machine in the hallway and if that memory still brought up a mix of good and painful sensations, it had to be the same for the people who went to Anderson.

In their case, though, there was no mimeograph, just an old coal stove that someone had to load every morning from November to April. I didn't know that when Mr. Woodson reached out though. I didn't know any of that.

. . .

Rufus Woodson came by my architectural salvage shop mid-morning on Tuesday in early July. It was already muggy in our part of Virginia, but I was refusing, as usual, to turn on the window unit in my small shed-turned-shop until it was really hot. Eighty-nine degrees and sixty percent humidity didn't count. Or so I told myself as I sweated through my button-down shirt while sitting in front of a fan.

My son, Sawyer, was oblivious to the heat, though, and he demonstrated his profound resilience by climbing a large, steaming mulch pile in the corner of the construction yard where I had my shop. Every few minutes, he'd come over and try to coax me his way for a demonstration, but I was unwilling to leave the fan and so said, again and again, "I can see you fine from here," which was the truth, if not the point.

So on this fine Tuesday morning when a man in a straw hat with a pristine white T-shirt and red suspenders came to my door and asked, "You Paisley?" I nodded, tried to look less sweaty, and said, "What can I do for you?" as I extended my hand to him. His dark brown skin was thick with callouses, and I knew instantly that this man had worked hard with his hands all his life. That automatically made him my kind of people.

Despite the fact that I had what some folks called a "fancy" college degree and had spent most of my adult years as a journalist, I had a special place in my heart for the people who worked with their bodies in jobs that went underappreciated. Maybe it was because I had never had to do that but had grown up with a father who had helped make his family's living by picking apples in the orchards. Or maybe it was just that I loved someone who appreciated hand-made things as much as I did. Whatever pleased me about calloused hands never failed.

"Paisley Sutton," I said.

"Rufus Woodson. I'm wondering if you might be interested

in a job." He smiled at me and then pointed at the air conditioner. "I'm pretty good with electronics. Want me to take a look?"

I blushed a deeper shade of red than the heat had already made me. "No sir. Thank you though. It works fine. I'm just—"

"Holding out. I get it. But let me tell you something, you can hold out too long for some things and never get to use them." He looked at the air conditioner again.

I got the hint, pulled the door closed after reminding Sawyer I was inside, and then turned the knob. The wave of cool air was instantaneous, and I felt like a fool.

Fortunately, Mr. Woodson appeared to be a kind man and didn't point out my foolishness. Instead, he said, "You familiar with the Anderson School up on Langston Road?"

I sat forward. "I am. Drive by it most every day of my life. Beautiful building."

"Yes, ma'am. Good memories, too, but it's got to come down before it falls down. Thought you might like to help us." He held my eyes as he waited for my answer.

"I absolutely would, but I hate to see it come down. It can't be saved?" A lot of the old schools around these parts had been fixed up as community centers or church fellowship halls, and I wondered if maybe that might be possible for Anderson.

He shook his head. "No. It can't. We looked into it. But there's a hole in the roof and a lot of water damage." He paused and looked down at the floor. "And enough hard things happened there that some folks would just rather see it gone now that it's on its way."

The reporter in me wanted to push at that statement, ask about what kind of hard things, but something in Mr. Woodson's carriage told me he wasn't inclined to talk about that with me or maybe with anyone.

"Tell me what you're thinking?" I asked. I'd long ago learned that some folks come in looking for favors, and some folks come in looking to do business. It was easier if I knew which I was facing before I started asking them questions.

"Some of us have gathered some funds, and we hope we might hire you to take down the building and salvage what is useful for us. Anything we don't want, you can have for free to sell here or use elsewhere." He looked up at me. "Would a thousand dollars do it?"

I smiled at the man. A thousand dollars would barely cover the cost of equipment, fuel, and crew, but I knew that if there was no organization or wealthy individual associated with this building, then it was just going to rot and fall in on itself if I didn't take this offer. So I nodded. "Of course it will. When do we start?"

His eyes softened. "I know that's not much, but—"

"It's plenty. And if I get a few things to sell and you get to use what you can, then it's well worth the work." I reached over and shook his hand to seal the deal.

"When are you available?" He asked as he stood. "We're pretty flexible in our retirement, but we would like to be there if that's okay."

"Ya'll good with a crowbar?" I asked.

He tilted his head and gave me the look Sawyer did when I asked something he deemed completely ridiculous.

"Alright then. I actually am free for the rest of this week, and if you and yours can be the crew, we can get started tomorrow." Normally, I used the construction crew for my friend Saul's business here on the lot, but I knew they were on a big house build over by the lake north of town this week. Saul, however, was free, having handed the foreman's job over to his best man. He'd been sulking around the lot for the past few days, so I figured I could get him over with a forklift to do the heavy stuff. Plus, he'd bring a truck and a trailer to load.

"Perfect," Mr. Woodson said with a smile. "I'll let everyone know. I expect you'll want to get started early. Beat some of this heat."

I sighed. I really enjoyed quiet mornings with a cup of coffee, Legos, and my four-year-old, but he was right. The day would be much easier if we could beg off by mid-afternoon. "That's right. Start at first light."

He nodded. "See you there at five forty-five." He tipped his hat and opened the door as I tried to suppress a groan at the idea of a five a.m. wake-up call.

I didn't have long to mope, though, because Sawyer came barreling in a couple of minutes later, his cheeks rosy and his hair sopping wet. In fact, his clothes were sopping wet, too, and as I watched, he dripped a fine pool of water on my shop floor. "Sawyer Sutton, what did you do?"

Before he could answer, a knock on the door preceded' Saul's entrance. "Sorry about the water, Pais," he said. "We had ourselves a good old water fight. Just sent him over to see if you had a change of clothes for him."

About a year ago, I had stopped carrying a diaper bag, and on an almost daily basis, I regretted that decision not to always have snacks, drinks, and extra clothes with me. Today was another day of regret. "I don't," I said, "but Saw, come on. I have some clothes I was going to donate to Goodwill in the back of the car. We'll find you something dry."

In the end, my son ended up wearing a blue and white, lace-shouldered shirt that I no longer liked the look of over top of his mostly dry Avengers underwear. He looked adorable, and thank goodness, he was completely unself-conscious because he paraded around the lot like he was the king of the world. Which of course he thought he was.

Saul got a big chuckle when Sawyer came around the building to where the older man was changing the oil on a bulldozer. "You are a sight, boy," he said.

"I'm dry, though," Saw said with a clear insinuation that he was far better off than his dear old and still wet uncle.

"You have a point," Saul said.

"You up to take down the old Anderson School this week?" I asked as I handed Saul a rag to clean his hands. "Rufus Woodson came by and asked for my help."

Saul wiped his hands and then dropped the rag in a plastic crate with a dozen others. "Sure. What's the arrangement?"

I told him about the plan to give most of the material to the folks who were funding the take-down and that we'd need to haul the lumber on his trailer to wherever they wanted it.

He nodded. "Sounds good." He narrowed his eyes at me. "They paying you fair?" His question was a legitimate one because it had taken me almost six months in this business to charge what my time and expenses were worth.

I shrugged. "Less than my usual but you know this kind of job, Saul. They want to pay, and they will pay what they can. The rest will shake itself out."

Saul nodded. "I do know." Saul was forever donating his equipment and his crew (with pay) for projects around Octonia County, so I knew he'd get it. "Okay, we starting early?"

I shuddered again. "Five forty-five."

He grinned. "Now you're getting it," he said.

FORTUNATELY, I have the best father and stepmother on the planet, and when I explained about our project at Anderson, they offered to have Saw spend the night and then come over to the job site with my dad about mid-morning. He'd been so excited that they came to get him right away That way, we could get some work done, Sawyer could get his sleep, and my stepmom would have a reason to try out a new pineapple pancake recipe.

This also meant that I had a night free and to myself, and so as soon they left, I texted my boyfriend, Santiago, to ask if he wanted to go out to dinner and a movie. As the sheriff of Octonia, he didn't always have nights off, but tonight, we had planned to watch TV after Sawyer went to bed since he was free.

When his response, *Adult or kid movie?* came through, I laughed.

Adult, I said. *Saw's staying with his Boppy and Baba.*

Oh, date night. I'll make sure I shower, he wrote back. *Pick you up at five?*

Perfect, I said. *Both the shower and the time.*

I could almost hear him laughing as we signed off, and it made me smile. I wanted to look nice for our date, so I grabbed a shower, put on a cute T-shirt dress I'd picked up on consignment, and slipped into my knee-high boots. Then, I placed a pillow case over one corner of the cat-fur-covered sofa and gave myself an hour to just sew.

I was working on a simple pattern now, a heart with headphones around it, because my friend Mary was a true music lover. I thought of her as soon as I saw the pattern, and I had vowed to get things for the people I loved when I saw them.

I'd started in the center of the ruby-red heart, and I thought that if I focused, I could finish it before Santiago came. I typically did much more complex patterns with lots of variation and shading, but this one was straightforward and minimalist. It was going to work up fast, which felt good given how much I had going on right now.

My new shop had taken off like a rocket, and I was to the point that between salvage jobs, keeping up with my research around those jobs, and running the shop, I didn't have a lot of time left for sewing. Fortunately, with more sales and jobs came more income, so I had just hired a part-time employee to run the shop.

Her name was Claire, and she was a senior in high school

who wanted to go to college to study architecture and history. She'd been into the store a dozen times since I'd opened, and she always had the best questions about where objects had been in a building, about what period they were from, and about how to take care of them. So when it had become clear I needed some help, she was my first choice.

Fortunately, Sawyer loved her, too, so we had worked out a salary of sorts that involved her hours at the shop – including two school days since she was getting school credit for this work based on a proposal she had written to her principal – and some babysitting time with Sawyer. She'd be paid well, and I'd finally be able to plan my schedule and stop relying only on my dad and stepmom to help with Sawyer. It was exciting for all of us.

But tonight, I was glad my son was with his grandparents, I was going to have a date with a man I loved (although I hadn't told him that yet), and I was able to get some sewing done, too. When I poured myself a glass of white wine as I sewed, it was the perfect beginning to the night.

The date was incredible, too. Santiago found this great farm-to-table place up in Culpeper, and then we slipped into the tiny theater there to see the latest Marvel movie. My boyfriend was usually pretty reserved, but when it came to superheroes fighting to save the universe, he actually threw air punches and cheered when the villains got their comeuppance.

After he dropped me off at home and gave me a pretty screen-worthy kiss goodnight, I climbed the stairs to my room, slipped into my pj's, and slept soundly until my alarm woke me at four-thirty. It was a rough start, but as I got into my old jeans and an old Relay for Life T-shirt, I felt my energy mounting.

A new building always meant exciting finds, be they architectural or historical, and either way, I knew I was in for a day of great stories, especially with Mr. Woodson and his friends. I had a whole list of questions for them, and I hoped they'd be willing to tell me about their time in the school while we worked.

As usual, Saul was on site before I was, and he already had the forklift ready to go. As I pulled up, Mr. Woodson climbed out of his car with another man and a woman who looked a bit too young to have gone to Anderson. "Paisley, this is my niece Jamila," he said as he came over and shook my hand. "And this is Foster Grant."

I shook everyone's hands and said, "Thank you so much for inviting me to work with you on this historic project. I'm honored, and I hope I can learn more about what it was like when you went to school here as we work."

Jamila smiled at me and let out a chuckle. "You'll be lucky to shut these two up," she said. "They've been telling me stories nonstop since we got up."

Rufus laughed. "We do have some tales, huh, Chucky?" He looked over at Mr. Grant.

"That we do, Roof," Mr. Grant said. "Nice to meet you, Paisley. We have a couple more folks coming, I believe. But we can get started whenever you're ready."

I glanced over my shoulder to where Saul leaned against the forklift tracks with a cup of coffee in his left hand. "I think Saul is ready. Come on. I'll introduce you."

Introductions made, Saul got right to work lifting off the roof while Mr. Woodson and Mr. Grant, who had insisted I call them Rufus and Foster, guided it to the ground with ropes. Then, as daylight arrived fully, two younger man and an older woman arrived in a gorgeous burgundy Cadillac. Rufus introduced us quickly and told us that the young men were here for their muscles and their brains, since both of them were studying structural engineering down at the University of Virginia.

"Awesome," I said. " We can always use some wisdom about how not to kill ourselves in this process."

The guys smiled and headed over to inspect the building while I talked to Shelley O'Hara, their grandmother. "Nice to meet you, Ms. O'Hara. Thanks for coming out."

"Please, child, call me Shelley. And thank you."

Jamila wandered over and pointed to the men, who were doing that thing I was getting so used to men doing. They had their hands on their hips, feet spread apart, and were all looking at the school building like they were disassembling it in their minds, which to their credit they probably were. "They need a minute," Jamila said.

I laughed. "Clearly. So maybe you can tell me, Shelley, about your history with the school?" I pulled my phone out of my pocket and held it up. "If you don't mind, I'd like to record what you say, too."

Shelley waved a hand. "Feel free, but I don't know that what I can tell you is worth recording."

I shook my head. "All of memory is worth recording," I said and was glad I already had the phone recording because that line was something I wanted to use again.

Jamila smiled. "Absolutely. Now, when did you start school here?"

"I went from first to eighth grade here. All the years we had at the time." She looked at the building and her face went soft. "It was a great place. Full of laughter when the teachers weren't pushing us to read and learn more. Then, it was all business. Not a one of those women brokered a fool, you know."

I nodded. "Education was serious business."

"Still is," Jamila said. "My four girls know that I take their learning as top priority, in all the ways."

"I know that's right," Shelley added. "We learned book stuff here, but also how to balance a checkbook, how to keep the building clean, and how to survive," she waved her hand behind her, "out here."

I had a lot of questions I wanted to ask, especially about

what Shelley meant about surviving out in the world, but I knew it was best to let the stories come as they would. People had a natural inclination to talk if they thought someone was listening, and I trusted that if I kept myself attuned, I'd learn a lot today.

At that moment, though, the men began to stir, and we took that as indication that they were ready to get to work. I was the one in charge here, and I knew that. Saul did, too, but I also knew that society being what it was, it was important for me to honor the knowledge of the men around us. They were good men, all of them, I could tell, but they were also men, and men had been taught that their value came from what they knew and what they could do. I didn't want to steal their sense of worth, but I wasn't going to let them run roughshod over me either.

"Alright, men, what's first?" I asked, looking at the college students for leadership.

One of them said, "Everything but that back wall looks pretty sturdy, so maybe we start there." He looked at his cousin and then over at me. "If that sounds good to you?" he asked.

"That sounds perfect," I said and then headed toward Saul, who gave me a quick single nod to confirm the guys' assessment. I was glad to see the young men knew what they were doing, but if Saul had balked even a bit, I would have suggested a discussion. He was the expert in all things construction and demolition. "Just give me a minute to determine what's inside that we want to salvage and then we'll get to taking down the building, if that suits you, Rufus."

He nodded. "Sounds good." He led the way to the building, and I asked him and Foster if it was okay for me to record while we walked. With permission granted, we stepped into the small foyer. "This is the coat room," Rufus said.

I noted the hooks on the wall and the low, rough-hewn benches. "What in here do you all want to salvage?" I asked.

Rufus looked to Foster and Shelley, "Do you all want any of this?" Both of them shook their heads, and Rufus said, "It's all yours, Paisley."

I smiled. "Wonderful. I'd like to salvage all of the benches, and if we can get the hooks off the walls with the board behind them intact, I'd like to have that, too." I looked around. "I think we can salvage the boards on the walls, too," I added. They looked to be knotty pine that had been whitewashed. "They're in good shape if you want them."

"Definitely," Grant said. "I think folks might use them in their houses and such if we offered them up for a good price."

Rufus nodded. "Maybe you could help us price them, Paisley?"

"Definitely," I said as we stepped into the first classroom. Immediately, I noticed the characteristically huge windows that allowed for a massive amount of natural light to come into the room from both sides. Then, I looked at the potbelly stove in one corner. It was in great shape, not a bit of rust on it. But it was the desks that most captured my eye. They were gorgeous with their patinaed wooden tops and green metal frames. As I walked around, I noticed drawings and etchings in the wood. "What about these? Do you want them?"

Shelley had moved over to stand beside one desk right near the stove. "I want this one," she said. "It was my desk." She ran her fingers along the wood and let them linger near the front corner, where the wood had broken off.

"Great," Foster said. "Maybe we could each take our own and then let Paisley have the rest?"

"No one else will want one?" I asked as I thought about all the other students who had attended here.

"No one else is here," Rufus said, "So they're all yours."

"Ah, we're operating on the 'finders keepers' policy," I said with a grin.

"Precisely," Rufus said as he began to move toward the front of the room. We spent the next half hour talking about where all the furniture and salvaged material were going to go, and from what I could see, we were going to be able to save most of the building except maybe the back part of the floor in the second classroom, where the water damage was just too great.

We carefully went over to explore that section of the floor with our engineers. They came with metal digging bars, and I was impressed. Those were the perfect tools to test the integrity of wood since their weight alone was enough to gouge damaged boards.

Very quickly we saw that the boards were rotted through, even though they still looked solid. One bang from the rod had a hole clear through the floor, and a couple more swift hits disintegrated a giant section from the very back corner. These boards were beyond salvage, even for burning maybe.

But a hole in the floor meant an opportunity for me to see what treasures might be beneath the building, so with permission of my hosts, I clambered down into the crawl space and shone my flashlight right into the face of a skull.

2

Unfortunately, I was a bit too seasoned at the "finding old bones situation", and I didn't even scream. I did, however, scramble back out of the hole quickly and shout for Saul. Something in the tone of my voice must have made him worry because he came running, and Saul didn't run.

"Tell me you didn't, Paisley Sutton," he said as he looked at me sitting on a solid piece of the floor near the broken boards. "Again?"

I sighed and nodded. "Can you call Santiago?"

He took out his phone and dialed as if by rote, which it might have been given how many times we'd now found bodies on job sites.

As he stepped outside, I told Shelley, Jamila, Rufus, Foster, and the students what we'd found. "It's quite old. But it's been well-preserved under the floor." I didn't want to tell them the body was definitely that of a woman, given the dress she was wearing, or that she also still wore her circular gold glasses. That felt like too much to reveal at the moment, what with the need to investigate and to honor the fact that this building held more than just good memories.

Rufus slumped into one of the children's desks nearby, and Jamila went to put her hands on his shoulders. The rest of us just stared at the floor and waited for the sound of sirens.

Fortunately, Santiago mostly used his sirens to entertain Sawyer, so he stepped into the room out of the near silence and said, "Thank you all for waiting." He cast a glance at me and held my gaze. When I nodded that I was okay, he proceeded in his professional manner.

"Please tell me what you found," he said with authority.

"There is a skeleton just about there," I pointed about three feet in front of me, "under the floor. I didn't touch the bones or get very close, but it looks like it's been there a while."

Santiago nodded. "Okay, I'll need to take a look, and Savannah is on her way. Can you folks stay around for a while so we can talk more if needed?"

Everyone nodded, and then I stood to lead us out of the building. "I have some camping chairs in the back of my car," I said. "Let me get them."

I was glad Santi's deputy Savannah was coming to join him, both because I wanted him to have support and because I liked her.

Within a few minutes, we were all seated. I had texted Mary and asked if she could bring over some iced tea since I knew she was home from work that morning, and she arrived in short order with plastic cups, fresh biscuits, and super-sweet tea, which was just what all our stymied systems needed. She dropped off our sustenance and headed to her job as a nurse. I made a mental note to take by a peanut butter pie from the Mennonite market to say thanks. She loved that pie.

Dad, Lucille, and Sawyer had been due anytime now, but fortunately, I caught them before they went out the door and explained, in brief, that it wasn't the best time for Sawyer to

come. The kid had already seen enough crime scenes in his
young life. He didn't need to add one more. They offered to
take him to Kings Dominion for the day, a trip they'd been
wanting to do for some time, and I readily agreed on the stipu-
lation that they remind him that eating too much junk and
riding roller coasters might not be a good combination.

As the sweet tea and biscuits with warm honey got into our
system, we all settled in a bit more, and when Savannah pulled
up and headed right into the building, we watched her with
steady eyes. It seemed we all agreed that this was going to be a
long morning and were resolved to it.

I had turned off the tape recorder before Santiago arrived,
but I took it out again with the hopes that maybe telling some
stories might distract us as we waited.

When I held the machine up, Rufus nodded and then, after
I'd touched the screen to begin recording, he said, "We thought
this might happen."

I nearly dropped the phone. "What do you mean?"

"There were rumors," Shelley added.

"But no one really knew," Foster said as he looked at the
younger people around them. "You all haven't heard, I guess."

The two young men and Jamila shook their heads. "What
are you talking about?" Jamila asked as she twisted her long
dreadlocks in her left hand. "You knew there was a body?"

Rufus sighed. "No, not exactly. We knew that Ms. Agee had
left, and some of us thought something had happened to her.
But we weren't sure."

"We were sure, Rufus. Let's be honest," Shelley said.
"Someone killed her. We all knew it. Our parents knew it. We
just didn't know any more than that."

I stared from person to person in the circle, and the three
elders looked decades older than they had just an hour before.
"Maybe you should start at the beginning," I said.

Shelley, Rufus, and Foster exchanged long glances, and

then Shelley began. "We were all in school at the same time, as you know. I was the oldest, in seventh grade, and these two were a year behind me." She pointed to the men across the circle from her.

Foster nodded. "That year made a big difference in lots of ways, but our teacher, Ms. Agee, worked hard to accommodate all of us with our different, um, struggles." He stared across the circle toward the building behind Shelley. "I had a big temper. All those hormones and my body was getting weird."

I smiled. "Puberty."

"Exactly," he said. "I just wanted to be outside and play in the woods, get away from all the massive feelings in me. But Ms. Agee stuck with me. She helped me focus, gave me extra time outside when I really needed it, and," he paused and swallowed hard, "she was the first person who told me there was nothing wrong with me when I said I liked Rufus here."

The two men took each other's hands, and I grinned. "You two have been together since sixth grade?!" I couldn't even imagine a love that long.

"Sure have. Never apart," Rufus said. "But you can imagine that back then, most people didn't like the idea of boys being together." He glanced at Foster. "Some still don't."

I huffed. "Yeah, I get it. That must have been really hard."

"It was," Shelley said. "Especially for Ms. Agee. She was already alone here, come up from Fluvanna to teach us, and then she had to deal with poor textbooks and all of us grades at the same time across two classrooms—"

"She taught everyone?" I shook my head. "I'd have thought you'd have a teacher for the lower grades and one for the upper, one in each room?"

"That's how it was supposed to work," Rufus said. "But when stuff got really going with Civil Rights, a lot of the teachers went South to help out with the voting brigades and Dr. King's work. One of our teachers even went out to California to work with SNCC – the student nonviolent coordinating committee. There just weren't enough local folks to teach us, and our parents couldn't afford to bring someone in from up north."

As I thought about how hard it must have been for those teachers to decide where to put their energy – the public fight or the quiet one of education – I realized there was a whole ton I didn't know about Civil Rights history. I'd have to learn, and quick.

"But Ms. Agee, she never complained," Foster continued. "She showed up every day to teach, and on the weekends, she was out in the streets marching and protesting with our parents. I don't know if the woman ever slept."

"She didn't sleep much, that I can tell you," Shelley said. "She lived upstairs at my parents' house above the kitchen. And I could hear her walking around up there all night long sometimes. Mama thought she was praying. I thought she was planning."

Jamila sat forward. "Planning what?"

Shelley shook her head. "I never knew. Just heard her one day when I was being nosy and climbed up the stairs to listen. Sounded like she was talking herself up for something, saying things like, "Hortense, you can do this. You can keep that school going. Now just think." And "Don't let those bullies beat you, girl." I never knew exactly what she meant, but she sounded scared but fierce, too."

"Someone was going to close the school," one of the students said.

Shelley shook her head. "I never knew nothing about that, but sounded like Ms. Agee thought so." She looked down at her hands. "I asked my parents about it one night at dinner when Ms. Agee was there, tried to make it sound like I'd heard about it from some other kid. But the three of them just looked at each other, and then Daddy told me to mind my own business. And that was that."

"He was protecting you," Rufus said with certainty. "He knew what was coming."

This time, I leaned forward. "What do you mean?"

He shook his head. "I don't know for sure, but about that time, my daddy pulled me out of school. Said I could go back when it was safe again but wouldn't tell me more." Rufus looked over at Foster. "Those were some hard days."

Foster squeezed his hand. "They were. Heard a teacher and some students over the mountain got burned up in their school. And our folks were scared to death. My mama let me stay, mostly I think because she had to work and worried more about me being home than about being with Ms. Agee at school. But she was worried, made me come straight to where she cleaned Ms. Jones's house after school."

"So you all think someone came after Ms. Agee because of what she was doing outside of school?" Jamila asked. "The protests and such?"

Shelley shook her head. "I don't rightly know, honestly. Could have been that. Could have been a lot of things." She let her eyes flick over to Foster and Rufus but quickly looked back at me. "No telling."

Foster spoke up. "I've always wondered if someone got wind of the fact that she let Roof and I spend time together at recess." He shook his head. "It was just innocent. Talking, holding hands. Nothing inappropriate . . . at least to good people."

Jamila put her hands on top of her head. "She was a woman ahead of her time, that's for sure. And that could be dangerous."

I nodded. "Sure could." I sat back in my seat and looked up at the sky. "Would you all mind if I asked Mrs. Nicholas at the historical society what she might be able to look up?"

Shelley laughed. "Look up? Girl, she went to school here,

too. She might just know." She looked over at Foster and Rufus. "Why didn't we ever ask her before?"

The men shook their heads and shrugged. "Sometimes maybe we just don't want the answers," Rufus said.

I started to ask if they still felt that way, but just then Santiago and Savannah came out of the building. They looked solemn, and while I hadn't expected jubilation at having just had to inspect a body, I was a little worried about just how serious they seemed.

"I can't tell you all much, you'll understand, not until we identify the victim and identify her next of kin—" Santiago began, but Rufus interrupted him.

"That's Hortense Agee, Sheriff, and she doesn't have any kin, as far as I know." Rufus's voice was firm and sure, and it answered my question about whether or not they were ready to hear the answers to their questions. "She was a teacher here. We all knew her." He looked from Foster to Shelley and back to the sheriff.

Santiago stared at the man for just a minute as he let what he'd just heard sink in. Then he said, "Well, I appreciate that information, but we need to have a solid identification before we can act on that information. She is just a skeleton, of course, but if you all would be willing to look at her, you might recognize something about her body."

I thought back to the wire-rim glasses and the long dress and felt sure they would know who she was immediately if it was, indeed, Ms. Agee. Everyone in the circle stood up and headed into the building, where the skeleton was now up on the floor under a sheet.

Savannah walked over to the body and said, "Are you ready?"

Everyone nodded, and Savannah gently lifted the sheet. It took only a matter of seconds before Shelley said, "That's her. That's Ms. Agee."

Savannah lowered the sheet back into place. "How can you be sure?"

"Those are her glasses," Foster said. "And she always wore dresses like that."

"And the pin," Rufus added. "The small silver A on her chest. She liked to wear it as her initial but also because she enjoyed the scandalized way that anyone who had ever read *The Scarlet Letter* looked at her. She was always one for stirring up trouble." Tears came to his eyes as he finished, and Foster took his hand again.

We stood silently for a few minutes, but then Shelley said, "I don't suppose you can tell us, Sheriff, but how did she die?"

Santiago sighed. "I'm afraid I can't tell you that, ma'am, but I can assure you that I will do everything I can to find out who did this to her."

Shelley shot Rufus and Foster a quick look, and my instinct was to ask what else they knew since that look definitely said they knew something. But we were now past the point of exploring history. We were trying to solve a murder, and that was not my role in this scenario. That place belonged to my boyfriend, and I had no doubt he had caught that look, too.

He didn't say anything, though, and if he wasn't going to ask, there was a good reason. So I stayed quiet and followed everyone out of the building again.

Saul, who had been tucked into the cab of his forklift with a Western novel this whole time, climbed down. "We're halted for a while?" he asked Santiago.

"I'm afraid so. But we won't hold you up long. With the roof gone and rain coming, we'll need to process the scene today. I don't expect we'll need much more time than that, so you can come back tomorrow to finish up." Santiago patted Saul on the shoulder. "Thanks for waiting."

"Anytime," he said and waved his book in the air. "Mama

taught me to come prepared for anything." Then he turned to our new friends. "I'm sorry for your loss."

I don't know how Saul knew that these people knew the victim, but his voice was sure. He had lived a long life of people underestimating what the construction guy understood, and I expect his years of observing while being treated as invisible had honed his ability to read people very well.

"Thank you," Rufus said. "We'll be back tomorrow. Need to finish this out right, especially now."

Santiago nodded. "I'll come along and help, if that's okay. And I'll keep this quiet as long as I can."

"Mighty nice of you, Sheriff," Foster said as he shook Santiago's hand. "We'll wait until we're done taking down the building and you give us the go ahead before sharing the news."

Shelley and Rufus nodded, as did Jamila and the two students. "See you in the morning," one of the boys said, and then the group of six walked back to their cars and drove away.

"Same time tomorrow," Saul said as he climbed back into his flatbed truck.

"Yep," I said. "Thanks, Saul."

He waved as he put the truck in reverse and pulled out.

Only when he got out of the driveway and Savannah went back inside to begin processing the scene did Santiago reach for me and pull me close. "You okay?"

I nodded against his chest. "I am. But I have a lot to tell you, and I don't think I know all of it yet."

"Not by a long shot, Pais. Not by a long shot," he said.

As Santiago went back in to help Savannah, I dialed Xzanthia Nicholas's number. I liked Shelley, Rufus, and Foster, and I had no reason to think they would do anything inappropriate here. But I also knew that grief and anger made people do things they wouldn't normally do. I needed to give my friend and the director of the historical society a heads up about the situation so that she could be prepared.

It was a risk to make the call since I knew Santiago would probably have preferred to talk to her himself, but given the slim possibility that Shelley, Rufus, or Foster were on their way to the historical society right now, I didn't think I had time to explain the situation, not when he had to explore a crime scene at the same moment.

"Xzanthia Nicholas, Octonia Historical Society," my friend said into the phone after the first ring.

"Hi, Xzanthia, this is Paisley. Do you have a minute?" My heart was racing, and I wasn't sure why. But this call felt really important.

She paused before answering. "Just a quick one. Someone just pulled up in front of the society here. What do you need?"

"Tell me about the car in front of the Society?" I asked on impulse.

This time her answer was given quickly. "Deep red Cadillac. How can I help?"

As quickly as I could, I told her about the body here at the school and who I thought had just pulled up to her office. I didn't have time to soften the blow about her old teacher, but I had gotten to know Xzanthia well over the past couple of years, and if there was anything she wanted most in the world, it was that the truth about history be told – and be told well.

"I understand," she said. "I will give them general information but not anything specific until I have the go-ahead from Santiago." Her voice grew more crisp and professional as she continued. "Thank you for calling. I'll look into the details of that matter for you right away."

Her guests must have walked in, so she couldn't say more. But I got her message loud and clear. She'd only tell her class-mates the big picture, but she'd dig in deep for me. I said a quick thank you into the phone before she hung up. Then, I went up to the door of the school and watched Santiago and Savannah do their work.

I knew better than to enter the crime scene again, but since I'd been on site all morning, I thought it might be helpful if I shared what I'd learned about the building and Ms. Agee as they worked. So I began a running monologue of everything everyone had told me about her, about the building, and about their time at the school.

By the time I had recounted everything I thought was relevant, they were moving into the other classroom just to take some pictures and look around. For lack of something else to say, I told them that each of the people that morning had claimed a desk and that I was taking the rest of them. I pointed out the words and initials carved into some of them.

Savannah stopped at the front of the room next to the desk that had been Shelley's and bent closer to the surface. "Oh yeah," she said. "I see things written here. Some initials and hearts." She smiled but then bent closer. "Sheriff, you need to see this."

He strode over from across the room and bent down. "HAA will die," he read out loud before he stood up and looked at me. "What was Hortense Agee's middle name? Do you know?"

I shook my head but took out my phone and pulled up a genealogy website. Within seconds of entering Ms. Agee's name and approximate age, I had his answer. "Anna," I said and then stared at him.

3

After that revelation, Santiago and Savannah went through the entire building photographing every angle of every desk and then loaded up Shelley's seat into the back of Savannah's cruiser. She was taking it back to the department offices to give it a closer look.

Now, Santiago and I were waiting for Saul to come back to the site with a box truck so we could load the rest of the desks and other furniture. Nothing else had stood out about the building for Santiago, and he didn't want to raise suspicions unnecessarily, so he had asked Saul to come help. He wanted to keep his word about having the building ready for demo tomorrow, but he also needed to examine all the furniture for markings. It was his strongest lead, he told me.

Besides the student desks, we had two old metal teachers' desks, a couple of bookcases, and the benches from the foyer. Nothing stood out on any of the other pieces, but it was definitely worth a good look to see if we saw anything else.

I supervised the loading of the furniture by Saul and the members of his crew he had called back in so that Santiago could get back to the station and begin his investigation by having a conversation with Shelley about her desk. I had told him about my call to Xzanthia and how Shelley's car had shown up there, and while he hadn't been, as I had expected, thrilled I had called without asking him, he had been happy to hear that Xzanthia had committed to keeping the details away from the people who, now, seemed to be potential suspects.

"I'll see you tonight?" I asked as he opened the door to his cruiser.

"Of course, you will," he said. "I need to hear about the kiddo's big day at the amusement park, and besides, it's pizza night." He gave me a quick kiss and got in the car.

I hadn't realized until that moment how nervous I was that he would be upset enough to cancel our weekly date with Sawyer, so when he confirmed he was coming like it was a given, I felt a surge of relief. I also felt a little ridiculous, but I'd never been in a relationship where a disagreement didn't become a big deal. It was going to take some getting used to, I guessed.

Now, though, I had to focus on guiding the guys on how to load the furniture so that it would be not only secure, which they could do on their own, but also protected. We didn't want to damage evidence or my future profits.

These men were used to heavy lifting, so when I asked them if they wanted me to take the drawers out of the desks, they actually giggled. "We've got it, Paisley," one of them said and jerked out the top drawer to get a better grip on the top of the desk.

As he did, I heard the rustle of paper and ran over to his side of the piece of furniture. There, in the drawer, were pieces of paper of all sizes. "Hold on a minute," I said, as I bent down and opened the three drawers on the right side. They were full of notebooks and papers, too. "Can you guys get the bookcases? I need to ask Santiago about what to do with this."

They nodded and headed across the room to grab the first

set of shelves as I took a picture and sent it to Santiago. "What do you want me to do here?" I added below the picture.

"Box it up. We can go through it tonight." He included a winky emoji, and I laughed. He knew I was always eager to look through old papers, and in this situation, my interest was sky-high.

"Will do," I replied and went to grab the two plastic totes I kept in the back of my car, just in case I found a lot of small things to buy at a yard sale or something. I wasn't always someone who thought ahead, but I was glad I had this time.

Within minutes, I had emptied both desks and had the guys load them. Most of the materials were in the one above the space where we'd found Ms. Agee's body, which led me to believe that she had used that desk as her primary work space. But there were a couple of bound books and a handful of papers in the other. I kept them separate in the totes and marked the top with masking tape and a label of which room they'd come from. My work wouldn't hold up in a chain of custody situation, I didn't think, but at least we'd have any information we might need as we looked through things.

Now, all I had to do was resist the urge to get started without Santiago. If I did, he'd be frustrated again, and I didn't want him to feel that way. Besides, I knew that any information he would glean that afternoon would be helpful in making sense of what we found in the papers.

So with my son happily occupied elsewhere, the shop closed for the day, and an intriguing story to delve into, I did what I normally did in these situations and headed to my best friend Mika's yarn shop downtown. Being the amazing person she was, she'd set up a little workspace for me in a quiet corner of the store, and, today, I was going to use it for research, right after I picked up our favorite subs from the amazing grocery store deli in town.

I texted Mika to let her know I'd be there soon with a late

lunch and a new mystery, and she sent back a wide-eyed emoji and a thanks with a request for a Dr. Pepper. "It has already been a day," she said.

"You got it," I replied and drove back into town to get our food and two Dr. Peppers because, well, I'd had a day already, too.

When I stepped into the yarn shop, I could see exactly why Mika needed the soda and wished I'd grabbed a fifth of bourbon, too. It looked like a tornado had blown through Mika's shop. Yarn skeins were everywhere, some half unwound, some just tossed to and fro around the store. "What happened?!" I asked as I stepped over a tumble of orange alpaca yarn.

"Twins, age six," Mika said as she set two partially unwound skeins onto the work table at the back next to several others. "Their mother thought it would be just fine to drop them off to look around while she got a coffee."

I groaned. "Why would she think that?"

"Apparently, she's seen Saw in here and thought his privilege extended to her own two hell-spawn." She winced. "Sorry, they were cute girls, but they simply would not listen to me. It's not their fault. Clearly, no one has ever told them *no*."

"Gracious. Alright, well, let's eat, and then I'll help you clean up while I tell you about my morning. Fortunately, it did not involve the twins of disaster," I said as I slid the unskeined yarn over on the table and set out our subs, the sodas, and the surprise treat of two Baby Ruth candy bars that I'd picked up.

"Bless you," Mika said as she sat down and went right for the candy bar. "Today, dessert needs to come first."

I laughed and opened my sub, feeling like I was good with the traditional order of foods for the day.

While Mika ate, I filled her in on the goings on at the school, what we had found in the desks, and our plans to sort Ms. Agee's papers that night. Then, as we cleaned up from lunch and began to reorganize Mika's store, I told her about

Shelley's visit to the historical society. "I get that she was curious, but doesn't that seem quick?"

Mika tucked skeins of thick, blue yarn back into the black plastic crate where they lived. "Maybe. It's hard to tell. You were already anticipating she'd go there, though, so maybe it was just the logical thing to do when her day got upended."

I thought about that for a minute as I sighed over several skeins of bamboo baby yarn that had come unfurled in a massive tangle. "You could be right. But with the desk, doesn't that make it more suspicious?"

Mika shrugged. "Or maybe she just knows more that she hasn't told you yet. You were just talking this morning, right?"

"Yeah, we were." I put the baby yarn into its basket and carried the whole thing to the table. "Hopefully, she'll tell Santiago anything she knows."

"And meanwhile, you can find out what you can." She waggled her eyebrows at me. "You ready to internet stalk a dead woman?" She winced again. "Sorry that sounded far more casual than I meant."

"I know what you meant. And yes, exactly. I've already found out a bit about her, so I should be able to dig up more." I picked up the last basket of mix-and-match yarn that the twins of destruction had toppled over. "I'll probably go over to see Xzanthia in a bit, too."

"Good plan. Mrs. Stephenson will be in soon – I called in reinforcements – so maybe I can join you over there," Mika said.

"Awesome. We can grab coffee on the way." The Dr. Pepper had given me a little jangle of energy, but I was never one to pass up a chance to get coffee.

As Mika began the massive job of winding the unsellable yarn for donation to the women who made hats for newborns at the

UVa Hospital, I took out my laptop and dropped into the wing-back chair that I loved most. A few quick searches on the genealogy sites gave me Ms. Agee's birth date, the names of her parents, and the locations where she had lived, all in central Virginia with the exception of her time at Hampton to get her teacher's degree.

But as Rufus, Foster, and Shelley had said, she didn't appear to have many living relatives, not even cousins as her parents had both been only children, too. She was, after her parents passed when she was twenty-five, alone in the world. I could understand, then, why she poured herself into her students and into activism. I expected her work filled some of the emptiness.

Despite the basic biographical information I located, I couldn't find anything else about Hortense Anna Agee. No mentions in family trees. No newspaper articles, at least in the bigger papers. No nothing. I sighed. It felt sad that someone who had meant so much to so many children had been left with only a few scant facts to remember her by.

Before I let the discouragement get to me too much, though, I decided to head down to the historical society. Mrs. Stephenson had come in a few minutes earlier and was already tackling the tangle of baby yarn while she tended to customers, so Mika and I headed across the street to the coffee shop to get our coffees and a tea for Xzanthia. She only drank tea, but we picked up a mint blend that I thought she'd like.

When we entered the old house that served as the society office, I took a deep breath. The smell of old documents always made me happy, so much so that I bought every candle that referred to old books or paper with abandon. This building was chock-full of scent and didn't even require a match. In fact, Xzanthia eschewed matches for obvious reasons.

"I'll be right with you," she said from the research room to the left of the entrance hall.

"Don't get up," I said. "It's just me and Mika. We'll come to you."

As we stepped into the room with the long table running down the center, I let out a hard breath. "You're on the trail, aren't you?"

Xzanthia nodded as she took the tea from me and set it carefully on the mantel away from all the papers arranged carefully in front of her. "I am, and I think you'll want to see what I've found." She gestured to the chair next to where she was sitting and then offered the one across the way to Mika.

I sat down, careful to put my coffee at the far end of the table, and then said, "Okay, so I was able to find her birth date, the names of her parents, and just a bit more about her, but I don't have anything about her time here locally."

"Good. Well, I mean, it's good because that I can provide," Xzanthia said as she picked up a stack of papers just in front of her. "These are the articles from the local paper about her. She came, apparently, in 1961 with her degrees from Hampton." She handed me one slip of paper.

"So this was her first teaching assignment?" I asked.

"It seems so," Xzanthia added. She slid another piece of paper my way. "She was very devoted, it seems, because the paper reports on her renewed contract every year."

"Which paper? *The Daily*?" Mika asked. "Wasn't that the white paper?"

"It was," Xzanthia answered, "and that's an astute question. Because Octonia has always been small, we've always had just the one paper. But for a while, once a week, they ran a Negro page with announcements for the black community."

I nodded. "I'm guessing they had good subscription numbers for that day," I said, having learned full well that most of the time things for black folks were about how they benefitted white people, not the black people themselves.

"No doubt, but it's good news for us because there's a fair

amount of information about Ms. Agee on those pages." Xzanthia handed me a few more pieces of paper. "Like this announcement of her engagement to a local boy, Terrance Harlow." She tapped on the picture of the young couple.

I leaned in closer to look and then took a deep breath. "They look so happy." I passed the article to Mika, and she smiled.

"They do, but it didn't last." Xzanthia slid yet another sheet of paper my way. "He broke it off just two weeks later."

"The paper reported that?!" Mika asked.

"It was a legal requirement to announce an engagement back then, and most folks did it in the newspaper. But did they also have to announce if the engagement ended?" I asked.

"No, they did not," Xzanthia said, "but given the way that Mr. Harlow ended things with Ms. Agee, it's no wonder it made the papers."

I picked up the paper and began to read aloud:

AT APPROXIMATELY 1 am on last Friday, the 11th, Mr. Terrance Harlow caused quite the ruckus outside the home of Mr. and Mrs. Humphrey Stone as he shouted, apparently to the woman who was recently betrothed to him. "Give me back my ring," witnesses reported hearing along with a series of hateful epithets and accusations against Ms. Agee.

THE NEXT DAY, Ms. Agee was not available for comment, but her host, Mrs. Stone stated that Mr. Harlow "does not deserve someone as kind and strong of heart as Ms. Agee. She is well rid of him."

"I AGREE WITH MRS. STONE," Mika said. "Good riddance."

"Indeed," Xzanthia said, "but it might be wise for you to

read this article as well, Paisley. It brings up some interesting questions."

I looked at the paper she handed me and read, "Local Teacher Goes Missing" in the headline. When I scanned for the date, I saw it was just three weeks after Harlow had broken off their engagement. "She went missing not long after," I told Mika

The article went on to explain that Ms. Agee had not arrived at school as expected on a Monday morning. She had been away to visit friends back in Fluvanna for the weekend, and the Stones had just assumed she had gotten a ride back for work on Monday. But after she didn't show for work, they drove down to Palmyra to look for her. Her friends said she had not arrived as planned on Friday and had assumed she had needed to stay back and work since she had done something similar in the past.

"She was missing two whole days before anyone knew," I said as I passed the paper to Mika. "I don't know much about finding missing people, but I do know that being forty-eight hours or more behind in an investigation might mean the difference between finding someone and not."

"In this case, though," Mika said as she handed the article back to me, "it wouldn't have mattered, would it? She was probably dead before the end of Friday."

I stared at my friend as the truth of what she'd said sunk in. "Someone killed her and hid her body on Friday afternoon? That's what you're thinking."

Mika nodded.

Xzanthia grabbed her laptop from the end of the table and put in a quick search. "I wondered," she said mostly to herself before turning the laptop to face us. "It was unseasonably cold that weekend."

I groaned. "Someone put her under the school, and she froze there, which kept anyone from finding her body until, well, today." I shuddered. I knew she was probably dead when the killer put her there, but still the idea of the poor woman lying under there and literally freezing up made my skin crawl.

"That is so creepy," Mika said.

"Very creepy. And very deliberate, it seems to me," Xzanthia said. "Weather forecasting wasn't what it is now, but folks knew when cold snaps were coming. Someone planned this murder, I expect."

I shivered again. "I need to let Santiago know what we found."

"He's on his way over," Xzanthia said. "I called him as soon as I put this all together. He just had to finish up an interview he said, and then—"

The chime over the front door sounded, and Santiago stepped into the room a moment after. "Got everyone up to speed?" he asked.

"I did. Thanks for giving me the go ahead to share it with Paisley," Xzanthia said and smiled at me. "I knew she'd be able to help us put this all together."

I sighed. "Sorry I didn't clear this with you first. I wasn't thinking."

He shook his head. "No need to apologize. I knew you'd be researching, and I appreciate everything you all have found. Catch me up?"

Xzanthia recounted what she'd just shared with us, and then he said, "So I need to find out if Terrance Harlow is still around." Santiago took out his notebook and began to write.

But Xzanthia stopped him before he got his note finished. "No death record on file yet, so he's still alive. Last location I can find for him is Orange County."

Santiago closed his notebook and said, "I believe you're even faster than Paisley at finding out this stuff." He smiled. "I'll get the specifics and head over there to talk to him tomorrow. Seems we have some things to talk about."

"Seems so," Xzanthia said as she closed her laptop. "I know you're in the midst of an investigation, Sheriff, but is there anything else you can tell us that might help us in our research?"

I looked from my friend to my boyfriend and felt a lot of gratitude that she'd asked the question I had always asked before. I didn't want Santi to feel pressure to tell me anything he couldn't reveal, but we were already this far in, and I hoped he might share more.

"Not much to tell, actually. She died from a blow to the head, but we don't know the details of the weapon yet. But from the intensity of the wound, I think it's probably safe to say she died instantly." Santiago rubbed his hand over his chin. "Whoever hit her, hit her hard."

I sat back in my chair and thought a moment. "So it probably wasn't anyone we were with today?" I asked, trying to choose my words carefully in case Santiago didn't want to give Xzanthia more information.

"No. It couldn't have been a child," he said. "This person was far too strong, and since the blow was to the upper part of the head, it's not the right angle for a child."

"Some kids are tall, though," Mika said.

"True," Xzanthia added. "I was over five feet eight inches in fifth grade. But I assure you, I didn't kill my former teacher, and I don't think any of my classmates did either."

Santiago nodded. "That's good to hear," he said with a smile. "But now I do need to ask you a few questions about Ms. Agee if you don't mind."

I stood up to leave, but Xzanthia waved her hand for me to sit down. "Stay. It's more information for your research, and if we're sharing information, we might as well share it fully." She looked back to Santiago. "Please ask your questions. I'll answer as honestly and completely as I can."

"Thank you," Santi said. "Please tell me what you remember about Ms. Agee."

"She was my teacher from first grade to fifth grade, and I adored her. It was she who inspired me to go into history. She told the stories of history like they were novels, and I couldn't get enough. Plus, she filled in the gaps that our school books left and encouraged us to always question anything we learned." Xzanthia looked down at the table. "'Children,' she'd say, 'Question everything. Question every little thing.' I took that lesson to heart."

I smiled. "Everyone loved her, it seems. Rufus and Foster said she was supportive of their relationship."

"In the appropriate way, yes. They were pre-teen boys, so of course she kept a close eye on them, but only the way she watched over all of us to be sure we didn't make choices we couldn't take back." Xzanthia stretched her arms over her head and then stood and began pacing beside the table. "But she was the most open-minded person I'd ever met up until that point. Nothing offended her except exclusion and hatred."

Santiago nodded. "Can you think of anyone who would have wanted to hurt her?"

Xzanthia stopped walking and looked at him. "A lot of people, Sheriff Shifflett. A lot of people."

I turned in my chair so I could see my friend where she stood behind me. "Because of her activism?"

"That and any number of other things." She began pacing again. "Ms. Agee made no secret of what she believed, and people took offense at just that attitude, let alone what she actually said. A black woman with the nerve to speak her mind at all, never mind in public? You'd have thought she was the devil himself." Xzanthia's voice had gotten louder as she talked, and now she was practically shouting. "They called her a troublemaker, accused her of stirring the pot just to get attention."

"Who is they, Xzanthia?" I asked quietly.

My friend seemed to return to her poised self at the sound of my voice, and she took a slow, deep breath. "Sorry to lose myself there a bit. I was furious when Ms. Agee disappeared. I was sure someone had run her off, but now that I know someone killed her . . ." She took another deep breath. "Alright, let me see who I can remember specifically."

For the next few minutes, she listed off the names of county politicians, prominent families, and even some members of the black community associated with the school. "They were most upset that she didn't put an end to the 'abomination'" she put quotes around her own words, "between Foster and Rufus. It wasn't their way, the church's way." Her voice had gotten a hard edge again, and I knew from previous conversations that the church had done its fair share of harm to Xzanthia Nicholas. It was no wonder she had some venom when they had harmed other people.

As she took her seat and smoothed her cream-colored sweater down across her stomach, Santiago said, "Most of these folks have passed on, I believe, but a few people are still around. I'll start asking questions after I go visit Terrance Harlow." He stood up and came over to where Xzanthia sat, looking calm but also a bit fatigued. "Thank you, Ms. Nicholas. You've been a huge help."

"Just catch who did this, Sheriff. That's all the thanks I need."

4

After we left the historical society with the promise to keep Xzanthia updated on anything new we'd learned, Santiago went back to his office, and Mika and I walked back to her shop. It was almost closing time, so I spent the next bit helping wind up the last of the unraveled skeins. Then, all three of us walked out together at the end of the business day.

Mrs. Stephenson was headed home to a dinner of fried chicken and mashed potatoes, she told us. "My husband doesn't cook that often, but when he does, it's a meal worth getting excited about." She grinned as she climbed into her car, and then Mika walked me to mine.

"You sure you don't mind me coming along tonight? I know it's your usual night with your boys," she asked.

"No, please come. The day has been hard for all of us, and it'll help for us to be together. You need anything from your apartment?" I looked up at the windows above her shop, where Mika lived.

"Not unless I need my lined pants to keep Beauregard from kneading holes into my flesh again." She laughed, but last time she'd been over my Maine Coon cat had spent a full thirty minutes working the top of her thighs until they were just the right "consistency" for him to lay down on. Then, he had refused to move all night.

"I can make no promises," I said as I opened the car door. "Just ride with me. Santiago can bring you home later, I expect."

"Sounds good," she said, and we drove out of town toward my little farmhouse. Sawyer and I had been living here over a year now, and while I had adored the house when we first got it, now I loved it even more as the flowers and shrubs we'd planted began to bring some color and shape to the stark gray house on the hill. But it was the garden I enjoyed most of all. We'd expanded the vegetable beds last winter, and, now, I had a thriving no-till garden full of the vegetables we loved. Most days we had enough of a harvest to share with Dad and Lucille as well as put some out on the make-shift roadside stand we had at the end of the driveway. It felt good to share with our neighbors, and while we never charged for the food out there, sometimes people left jam or other goodies as a thank you.

As we pulled up, I stared at the daylilies and yarrow blooming by the porch, and I could see the nasturtiums and alliums out in the garden. I felt something of the weight of the day slide away in this peaceful place and said a silent prayer of gratitude. "Want to pick some veggies for the pizza? I think we have some jalapeños ready."

"I'm on it," Mika said as she grabbed the harvest basket off the porch and headed through the garden gate. I could hear her whistling as I let myself into the house and took a deep breath. Lately, I'd been interested in candles that had what some might call a more masculine scent, and so my house smelled of leather with a hint of cinnamon. It was lovely.

I grabbed the ball of homemade pizza dough from the fridge where I'd had it thawing since yesterday and divided it before working it into two pies, one for each of the fancy pizza stones Santiago had gotten me for my birthday. Then, I fixed up a batch of white pizza sauce to go with the fresh red I'd made over the weekend from our own tomatoes. I was just spreading the sauces when Sawyer burst through the door.

"Pizza night," he shouted. "I'm ready to help." He grabbed a chair from the dining room table and slid it over to the counter. "Where's the cheese?"

My son had become a regular chef in the past few months. He could mix his own pancakes, prepare chocolate milk, and even crack eggs with minimal shell intrusion. But pizza night was by far his favorite because he loved spreading the cheese. And by spreading, I mean *spreading* all over the pizza and the counter and just enough on the floor that Beauregard got a little treat if he hung around, which he always did.

"Where's your Boppy?" I asked as I watched my son sprinkle fresh, shredded mozzarella onto each crust.

"He said hi to Mika and then he and Baba left for their date." He looked up at me. "They're going to see the new Spiderman movie."

I was absolutely sure that I heard a bit of reprimand in his tone and made a note to check show times for Friday afternoon. It wouldn't be a bad thing at all to have Sawyer's first movie in the theater be a superhero one.

Just as we finished up the cheese, Mika and Santiago came in with arms and a basket full of vegetable goodness, including three jalapeños, which I needed for our jalapeño and honey pizza. I'd picked up that recipe from a local brewery, Bald Top, and it was my new favorite. They made it with pepperoni, which was delicious, but here, I just kept it vegetarian and left a couple of pieces without the spice for Saw.

After giving Santiago a brief kiss, I put him and Sawyer in charge of the white pizza toppings and grinned when they put on tomatoes, green peppers, and ham. As Saw ducked into the pantry for the can of pineapple I'd begun storing there, I asked Santiago about the rest of his day.

"Well, my conversation with Shelley didn't reveal much beyond what she told you. She says they knew something had happened to Ms. Agee, but they were just kids and didn't know what to do." He looked puzzled. "She did say that her dad had acted kind of hostile about the whole situation when she'd asked him about it back then, and so she finally just stopped asking since it wasn't doing any good anyway."

As Sawyer carefully drained the juice from the pineapple, I laughed. "Maybe her dad just got weary of not being able to help?" I certainly understood that feeling as I watched my formerly clean counter become covered in pineapple juice but held my tongue.

Santiago nodded. "Could be." He went back to helping Sawyer spread toppings on what was now definitely *their* pizza. That was a combination of foods I just couldn't enjoy. "But I did locate Terrance Harlow. He's over in Rapidan. I'm heading there in the morning."

"That's good news," I said. "He's a suspect then?"

"Yeah, at least until I hear what he has to say." He gave Sawyer a high five and then opened the oven to slip in both pizzas before setting the timer so we'd remember to switch the shelves when they were halfway through baking.

"Saw, want to go swing?" Santi asked. "I'll push you big high."

Sawyer didn't answer but sprinted out the back door toward the swing his grandfather had fixed in the large pecan tree out front.

"See you in a few," I said as I watched my boyfriend follow my son. It was a good view.

As Mika poured us each a glass of wine, the text chime on my phone sounded. A message from my good friend Mary.

Is Santiago with you? Someone just told me something I think he needs to hear.

He's here. Want me to get him?

Mind if I come over? I have salad.

Come on. Pizza will be ready in ten.

With her salad, I thought we had enough for five, especially if Sawyer decided he hated pizza, per his usual.

She said she'd be over in a minute, and after I filled Mika in, I headed out to tell Santiago that Mary was on her way with some news she wanted him to hear. Sawyer was bumping into the branches at the top of the tree and giggling and Santiago dodged and weaved around his swinging body. They were having so much fun, and it was just the kind of fun that wasn't natural to me, that bodily stuff. I was glad Saw had Santi, as well as his dad, to play with that way. I was more of the books and Legos sort.

My message delivered, I headed back in to set up the TV tables on the porch and pull the camp chairs out of my car for the second time that day. My dining room table would fit us all, but the day was cooling off and with the fan on, the porch would be lovely. Plus, this way, Saw could run and play while we ate and talked. That seemed wisest given our topic of conversation and the remaining energy of a four-year-old after a long day.

Mary arrived with more than what I would call a "salad." I would use the term "salad bar" since she came in with two totes full of toppings, lettuce and spinach, and two kinds of dressing. "You had this just ready to go?" I asked.

"I do salads for lunch, so I prep all this the weekend before. Makes it easy to be healthy," she said with a smile. "Also makes me feel less bad for the nachos and cheese I often eat for dinner."

"I like your style," Mika said as she helped set up the fixings bar as I took the pizzas out of the oven.

Sawyer got his special fruit punch to drink, and the rest of us supplemented our wine with glasses of water brimming with ice. It was still summer in Virginia after all.

With our plates full, we headed to the porch, where Saw ate one bite of pizza, shoved a piece of lettuce into his mouth, and then went off to play some elaborate game with rocks, a homemade catapult, and a nearby tree.

Since the young one was out of earshot, Mary said, "Do you all know Marvin Simon?"

I looked at Santiago and then Mika, but we all shook our heads. "Who is he?" Santiago asked.

"He's a deacon at church. You've probably seen him, Pais. Sharp dresser. Always in pinstripe suits and a hat with a feather," Mary said.

"Oh yeah, I have seen him." The dapper man always caught my eye because not only did he dress well, but he moved like he knew it, too. Not arrogant but confident.

"Well, he texted me tonight to ask if I'd heard about what happened over at the school." She raised an eyebrow and looked at Santiago. "Word travels fast, huh?"

Santiago clasped his hands together on the top of his head. "I'll say. We had an agreement not to say anything." His hands fell into his lap. "I guess that was too much to hope for."

I reached over and took his hand. "It is Octonia. Word burns through ears like fire on tissue paper." I squeezed his fingers and then looked at Mary. "What did you tell him?"

"I played dumb, sort of. I mean I don't know what really happened, but I know something did, something bad since you were there, Santi. No offense."

He waved a hand in the air. "None taken."

"He said they'd found a body of one of the teachers, one of his teachers. He wanted to know if I knew what was happening now." Mary took a bite of her pizza and looked at Santi.

"We're investigating a murder," he said simply.

Mary chewed a minute and then said, "Of Ms. Agee?"

Santi looked at her for a long second and then nodded.

"I think you need to talk to Marvin then. He hinted that he knows something, but he didn't want to tell me." She took a sip of her wine. "I was fine with that. I don't need to know anything people are trying to keep secret. Too much trouble."

I smiled at my friend. "Tell me about it." I took a sip of wine, then said, "I know you didn't go to Anderson, but did you know much about the school?" Mary had grown up in Octonia, and she was a well-known voice in the black community here. If anyone knew rumors, she would.

"There have always been stories about the school. Mostly good ones. Lots of folks who loved that place, wanted to preserve it. Rufus Woodson wasn't particularly active in trying to save it, and I always thought that was weird since he seemed to love that building.

"He's the one who came to me to ask me to help them," I said as I tried to puzzle through everything. "He said he had wanted to save it, but the process took too long and now it couldn't be saved."

Mary nodded. "That seems about right. There were some fundraisers in the early 2000s to try and raise the money to fix it up, but folks just didn't give much. It was strange. We've raised a lot of money for things and people we care about in the past twenty years, but this one just didn't work." She shrugged.

I finished my first slice of pizza and went in for a second as I pondered what Mary had just said. "Did you notice that there was anyone actively *against* fixing up the school?"

"No, that's the thing. I didn't. I'd have known if someone was trying to have it torn down or left to rot intentionally. This was more of a quiet resistance, just like an energy that made people not want to do anything." Mary shook her head. "It doesn't really make sense."

"Unless a lot of people knew something that they weren't

willing to talk about and were protecting someone," Mika said as she sipped her wine and raised her eyebrows.

Mary studied her for a second. "I guess it's possible that there was some big secret people weren't sharing; something everyone quietly agreed to keep quiet." She shrugged. "But if that's the case, I never heard any hint of it at all."

I remembered when Rufus came to the store, what he'd said about some people really wanting the building to come down. The question, then, was, was it the people who wanted the building torn down who were trying to cover something up or the people who lobbied for it to stay standing?

THAT QUESTION, though, wasn't one I could answer tonight, and when the little man finally ate most of a piece of pizza and then curled up in my lap, everyone took that as their cue to help me tidy and head out. Santiago lingered a second after Mika headed to his car. "Think about sewing tonight, okay, Pais? Research can wait until tomorrow." He kissed me and then walked out the door.

Sawyer was asleep before I finished reading *Edward the Emu*, and when I went back downstairs, I thought about Santi's suggestion and decided to give myself permission to just relax. I turned on *Roswell* and decided to put Mary's project aside temporarily and let myself stitch on my new project for the house, a landscape of trees against a black background. I'd found the pattern on a new favorite Etsy shop, Satsuma Street, and I thought it would be a great piece for our living room as well as a fun project to help me look forward to autumn. So I picked up the orange thread and let myself wonder if Max and Liz were actually ever going to be together. It was lovely.

. . .

THE NEXT MORNING, Sawyer and I headed over to the school site. Santiago and Savannah were both going to be there, and Santi had assured me that one of them could keep an eye on Saw when I was busy. Saul would be around early as well. I would have asked Claire to watch him, but today she was working her last shift as a lifeguard at the pool so she could help me more regularly. So he was with me, at a murder site, again. At some point, Saw was either going to need therapy for this, or he was going to make something amazing from the experience. Maybe both.

But I should have realized that the minute he saw Saul and his forklift, I didn't need to worry that Saw would be anywhere near anything as unsavory as the talk of Ms. Agee's murder. Nope, he was in his Uncle Saul's lap in a flash, and Saul was grinning ear to ear as he let the boy steer the lift around the empty field beside the school. I breathed a sigh of relief. One stressor lifted.

As soon as Shelley's and Rufus's cars entered the field, though, my shoulders tightened again. The questions from last night were swimming around in my head, and while Santiago was going to follow up with Marvin Simon today after he visited Terrance Harlow, I had to figure out a way to keep conversation going, not reveal anything anyone wasn't supposed to know, and also get any information that might be useful to Santiago's investigation. Obviously, he hadn't asked me to do that last thing, but I knew I wouldn't be able to help myself, not when history and stories were involved.

We all greeted one another, and the engineering students led the way in to the back wall, where we would begin to remove boards and place them in a stack so Saul could load them onto his truck. With all the furniture gone, there wasn't much left to take down inside, so the men started on the wall while Jamila, Shelley, and I pried off the old chalkboards from the classrooms and the board with the coat hooks from the foyer.

The silence was fine for a bit, but then it began to feel awkward, like we were all carrying around something heavy as we tried to work. I decided to break the ice. Unfortunately my choice of ice breakers was a bit loaded. "So what do you make of what was carved in your old desk, Shelley?"

Fortunately, she didn't seem put off by the question, and she definitely didn't get defensive, which I took as a good sign. "I have no idea. I was the last person to sit in that desk, as far as I know, but I don't have any memory of that being carved there."

Jamila looked at her. "Wait, what did I miss?"

"Oh, right. Someone carved 'Die HAA' in the top of my old desk," Shelley said as she put a little more muscle behind the pry bar and popped one of the hook boards off the wall. "Clearly, it was a threat."

I sighed. "I've been wondering that. If someone wanted to scare her, wouldn't they have written that where she would definitely notice it. Like on her desk or the chalkboard or something."

Shelley tilted her head. "Good point. But why write it at all if it's not a threat?"

"A doodle?" Jamila said. "Someone was thinking about that and just carved it without consciously choosing to?"

"But who would have done that on *my* desk?" Shelley asked.

I pondered her question for a minute, but then said, after looking at Jamila, "You realize neither of us was even alive when that happened, right? How would we know?" I kept my face deadpan as she turned to me.

Then, she broke into a laugh and said, "Go on with you, child. Teasing an old woman."

From then on, the mood was light. We finished taking down the hooks and then the chalkboards, and then we helped the men get the rest of the boards off the back of the building. By the time we'd completed that task, it was time for a break, and we all sat down to enjoy the bottles of water I'd packed.

We'd all worked hard, and we were all due a rest. But I was very impressed with the stamina the elders among us had. They looked like they might outlast the engineering students, who seemed to have spent far more time with computerized buildings than real ones. They each chugged two bottles of water and then sprawled out on the grass.

"Got to get in shape, kiddo," Rufus said to one of the young men as he nudged his leg with his foot. "We're going to need you if we're going to build that community center over by the VFW."

I turned to Rufus. "You're going to build a community center?"

"Just decided last night. In honor of Ms. Agee," Foster said after taking a long sip from his water. "Seems like the right thing to do."

"Already got a couple of big donations just from our phone calls last night," Rufus said.

I stared at him a minute. "You called people about building a community center to honor Ms. Agee last night?" I studied him a minute longer. "After you committed to Santiago that you'd keep the news quiet?" I could feel the anger rising up the back of my throat. This kind of thing could put Santiago's investigation, not to mention Santiago himself, in danger.

Rufus sat forward. "Now wait just a minute. I saw the post on Facebook from Marvin Simon and thought the sheriff had decided to share the news." He looked at me closely. "Are you saying the sheriff didn't approve releasing this information?"

I threw myself back in my chair. "No, he didn't. But I'm glad to hear you weren't the source."

"Oh dear. No, I'm so sorry. I didn't realize . . ." Rufus let his head fall toward his hands.

"We never would break our promise to the sheriff," Foster

said as he put his hand on his partner's back. "But if the sheriff didn't tell him, how did Marvin know?"

I shook my head.

"Aunt Shelley, do you know something?" Jamila asked.

I looked over at the older woman, and she had the same expression Sawyer had when I caught him in a lie. Her eyes were wide, but she wouldn't meet anyone's gaze.

"Aunt Shelley?" Jamil asked again.

"I didn't think he'd say anything," she finally said quietly. "I just needed to talk about it with someone, and I knew Marvin would understand."

I groaned and typed out a message asking Santiago to call me ASAP. I wanted to rage and shout at her, but I knew that the word was out now with no way of pulling it back. I took a deep breath and asked, "Why did you think he'd understand?"

Shelley shook her head. "He and Ms. Agee were close. I knew he'd want to know we'd found her. He always believed something bad had happened to her."

"Some people said they were too close, if you know what I mean," Foster added. "He was seventeen, but still."

Jamila leaned toward the center of our small circle. "Are you saying that she and Marvin Simon were having a relationship?"

I couldn't read by the tone of her voice what Jamila thought of that possibility, but I was having to actively tap down all the thoughts of statutory rape and inappropriate relationships that I'd known about in my own life. "Were they dating?"

Rufus sat back. "I don't know. Seemed kind of like it sometimes, but he wasn't her student anymore, had a job for himself and all that. And no one ever saw them together," he said.

"Unless someone did," Foster added quietly.

"People didn't like the fact that they might have been together?" Jamila asked.

Shelley said, "Most people didn't care much. They were a

few years apart in age. And Marvin was a good kid, and as we've said, everyone loved Ms. Agee."

"But someone did care?" I asked.

"A few people," Rufus said. "Including my daddy and Shelley's daddy. They both thought it wrong for a teacher to date a former student, said it gave the other children ideas."

Shelley sucked her teeth. "My parents were good people, but my mama had some backwards ideas." She looked from Rufus to Foster. "I'm sorry she caused such a mess for you two."

Foster shook his head. "Water under the bridge and not your responsibility either, Shelley."

"Your mom didn't approve of Rufus and Foster being together?" Jamila asked.

"Not one bit. She'd take her lunch break and sit outside the school to see if she could catch them holding hands and such. Then, if she did, she'd read them the riot act and threaten to call the police." Shelley's voice was hard. "They were just boys."

"Your mama had some misguided notions, Shelley, but like Foster said, that's all in the past. Don't think no more of it," Rufus said as he reached over and took the woman's hand. "We're all here now, and that's what matters."

I had so many things I wanted to ask about, but the one that felt most pressing pushed its way to the surface. "What did Terrance Harlow and Marvin Simon think of each other then?"

"Oh, girl, that was some bad blood," Shelley said. "Real bad blood."

5

For what I could only imagine were our own reasons, we stopped talking about Ms. Agee's murder when we went back to work a few minutes later. For my part, I didn't want to delve too far into a discussion of Harlow until Santiago was there. He had texted to say he would be there in twenty minutes a few minutes after we started work and asked if I still wanted him to call. I told him no, that we'd just talk when he arrived.

And when he and Savannah pulled up a few minutes later, I met them outside and relayed our conversation from earlier. "Does any of that line up with what Harlow told you?"

Santiago nodded but then looked back at the building. "I'll tell you about it later."

Rufus and Shelley were standing in the doorway, and while I didn't think they could hear us from where they were, I knew that if Santi didn't want to take any chances, there was a good reason.

"Sounds good. You staying?" I asked.

"Well, I don't normally dress this way on the job, so yeah,"

Savannah said as she waved a hand in front of her torn jeans and tank top. "Where do you need me?"

I led them back toward the building and said loudly, "Who's up for a little men versus women contest?"

"I am," a tiny voice said behind me as Sawyer charged his way through my legs and into the room. "I have my hammer."

Everyone erupted into laughter, and I grinned. "Alright, Saw, you and the other guys get to work on the walls in this room. The women will take the larger room and be back to help you finish yours."

"Oh, woman," Shelley said, and then grabbed Savannah by the arm as they went into the room. "You do the main pulling, and I'll get the last part and stack. Work for you?"

"Yes, ma'am," Savannah said.

And with that, the four of us went to pulling down boards as fast as we could. As soon as we got a good pile, Jamila or I ran it out to Saul, who was loading things onto his forklift for us. Then, we'd go back in, pull some more, and repeat.

Within an hour, both rooms were completely stripped to the studs, and we were all soaking wet with sweat. The guys had won, of course, since there were more of them in the smaller room. I had been hoping that the presence of a toddler might slow them down, but instead, Saw proved himself quite the prybar expert.

"Losers buy lunch," I said, "by which I mean, lunch is on me."

"Too late," Foster said. "I have the Lafayette bringing us all burgers. They'll be here in five minutes."

"Did you get French fries?" Sawyer asked as he looked up at the older man.

"Sawyer Sutton, we don't ask for more when people are giving us gifts. You know that," I said.

Foster grinned at me. "It's no problem; I like a man who can ask for what he wants. Yes, sir, I did order fries plus

ketchup and garlic aioli for the grown-ups." He tousled
Sawyer's hair.

"I hate ketchup, but I love garlic ee-i-ee-i-o," Saw said with a
smile.

Foster howled with laughter. "Excellent. Want to help me
get the table out of the car?"

"Of course, I do," Sawyer said and took Foster's hand before
leading him toward the cars.

The food arrived, and we all sat around in silence as we
consumed more than enough calories to replace those we'd
burned off that morning. It was amazing, and the raspberry
lemonade that the Lafayette delivered was just the right drink
for this brutally hot mid-day.

"We don't have much left to do, folks," I said. "I'm thinking
we tackle the interior walls today but leave the floor for tomorrow. Sound okay to everyone?"

Heads nodded, and as soon as we had cleaned up from
lunch, we made quick work of the two long walls and the small
one in the foyer. The plaster and lathe made a huge mess, but
beneath, we found some solid studs that they could use for the
new community center. Plus, now, the floor should come up
easily since some of the boards had run beneath the wall. That
would be quick work for tomorrow, and today, we had done
plenty.

As soon as everyone had packed up and headed home, I
suggested to Savannah, Santiago, and Sawyer that we grab
some ice cream, and the shouts of enthusiasm were almost as
loud from the adults as from the child. We made our way out to
the Tastee Freeze and savored our dipped cones as we sat in the
shade of a nearby tree.

I so wanted to ask Santiago about what he had to tell me,
but since he didn't bring it up, I figured it might not be information fit for small ears and focused on enjoying the impromptu
outing instead.

When we were done, Santiago said he was taking the rest of the afternoon off if Savannah didn't mind, and when she assured him she had the next shift under control and would call if she needed him, she took the cruiser back to the station while Santiago rode with us to the house. We had an afternoon of weeding under the sprinkler ahead of us.

By the time the beds were weeded, we were all blissfully exhausted, soaked through to the skin, and ready for some videos and dinner. I popped some chicken nuggets in the oven and boiled the water for macaroni and cheese while Santiago grabbed a quick shower and redressed in the spare clothes he now kept in a drawer in my dresser.

I took my turn in the shower while Sawyer and Santiago finished up supper by making some peas. It was amazing how much more prone Saw was to eat something if he cooked it, so I was in for having him cook as much as was safe for him. It made us both happy.

Unfortunately, bath time didn't go as easily as dinner time, but with a little coaxing from Santi, the final one of our trio got cleaned up and off to bed where Santiago told him a story from his Abuela. Saw loved the story and wanted another, but when I said it was time to sleep, he curled up against Santiago in my bed and drifted off.

I so wanted the three of us to stay up there and sleep the night away, but Santi and I weren't there yet in our relationship. Plus, I really wanted the update on what had happened with Harlow and Simon. So we tucked Sawyer in and went downstairs to a glass of cold Chardonnay each.

With Santi propped in the corner of the couch and his feet on my lap so I could give him a foot massage, he started to tell me about his day. "Harlow is a piece of work, I'll tell you," he said. "Big guy. Must be six-foot-seven. Broad, too. Probably could have played professional football just because of his size, if he'd had the chance."

I nodded as I worked the arches of his feet, and he groaned a little in pleasure.

"It's easy to think a man that big is going to be rough, but he wasn't; pleasant as could be. Invited me in for iced tea and then told me he figured I'd be coming by since he'd heard they'd found Hortense. 'Seeing as how we were going to be married and all, and I kind of lost my mind for a minute.'" Santiago imitated the man's voice by dropping his an octave and speaking more quietly.

"Wow. So he was upfront with you?" I said as I rubbed the back of Santiago's ankles in the spot that always hurt me the most.

"Completely. Said he had indeed gone to the Stone's house and made a scene. He was lost in grief, he said. He'd just heard that she was cheating on him with a former student, and he was furious and hurt. 'Out of my head,'" he said.

"He knew about Simon?" I asked.

"Yep. Said his daddy told him that he'd seen his teacher walking with that boy on the road and that there were walking *real* close." Santiago shook his head. "It's amazing what jealousy can do to a person."

"Now, Santi, you know Saul and I are just friends," I teased as I rubbed the balls of his feet and watched my boyfriend melt further into the cushions.

"Very funny," he said with a wink. "But I didn't get the sense that Harlow stayed mad long. He was hurt, sure, but he said the next Monday he stopped by the school before it opened and apologized to Hortense, told her he understood and that he wished her the best."

I frowned. "That's awfully big of him, but if he was going to be so chivalrous, why ask for the ring back? I mean, he probably had a right to, but why in *that* way with all the shouting?"

"I asked the same question, and apparently that was his mama's notion. She told him that Hortense owed him that ring or the money for it right away. She had some strong feelings herself about the woman who broke her son's heart." His eyes closed, and he let his head fall back.

I continued to rub his feet as I thought about what I would do to the first person who broke Sawyer's heart, and I only realized how far I'd gone into my revenge fantasy when Santi jerked his feet away with an "ouch." "Sorry," I said. "Well, what's your read on Harlow?"

"I don't see him doing this," Santi said. "He's been married fifty years now. Seems quite happy." He sank back into the couch again. "Now, Simon on the other hand."

"Oh yeah?" I asked as I moved to slide my legs over his in a not-so-subtle hint at my own foot rub.

Santi smiled and picked up my right foot, and I oozed down further so he wouldn't have to reach. "It was like a study in contrasts. Simon is small, skinny -- built like Dave Chappelle but with no sense of timing. He was so nervous that his hand was slick when I shook it."

"What did that tell you?" I asked.

"That kind of nerves comes only when you've got something to hide, in my experience. So I tried to keep him off kilter and asked about his affair with Hortense Agee." Santiago smiled.

"Just like that, first thing?"

"Yep, and it worked. He told me that he had had a big crush on her but that it wasn't anything more than that. 'I swear,' he must have said about a dozen times."

I switched my feet in Santiago's hands and said, "Methinks the man doth protest too much."

"My thoughts, too, but I couldn't get him to change his story, no matter how hard I tried. I even told him about Harlow's father seeing him and Hortense walking along the road, but he said that was just her coaching him about maybe going to college. Nothing more." Santiago shook his head. "He's definitely hiding something, but I'm not sure that it was that he and Hortense Agee were a couple."

"No? What could it be then?" I asked as I sat up.

"That's what I've got to find out." He slid over and put his arm around my shoulders. "But for now, what do you say we watch Bake Off?"

"I love you," I said as I grabbed the remote. "It's biscuit week, you know."

"I do love a biscuit," he said as he winked at me. "Mind if I crash in Sawyer's bed? I don't really have a way home."

I blushed. I so wanted to invite him upstairs, but our first night together in my bed probably didn't need to involve a toddler. "Absolutely." I kissed him quickly and then changed the subject. "You do know—" I started.

"Yes, I know that the British call cookies biscuits. I love cookies, too."

THE NEXT MORNING, the shop needed to be opened, and while Claire was planning on being there for the day, I needed to also be on site to help her learn the ropes. She was all up to speed on the register and the inventory, but her nerves were still up about guiding customers. I'd told her I'd be on hand today to give her some tips but that tomorrow, she was on her own.

The problem was, of course, that I also needed to be at the school to help take up the floor. I decided I could spend a few hours at the school and then head to the shop to help Claire open at ten. With any luck, we'd be pretty much done at the school before I needed to leave, and if we weren't, then Saul could supervise the final stages of clearing the joists and such.

With that plan in mind, Sawyer and I ate the oatmeal he made for us, and then we loaded up. Sawyer had the brilliant idea of taking his balance bike along so he could ride around while we worked, and so I opened the back to load it in. That's when I found the two totes of papers from Agee's desk. In the flurry of activity the past few days, I'd forgotten all about them.

I took a quick picture and texted it to Santiago. *We forgot*, the message said.

Doggone it, he replied. *We need to look at those.*

Agreed. Want me to bring them by?

Nope. If you're up for it, we can sort this afternoon at your store.

Sounds good. Then, Indian for dinner?

Only if we get a double order of samosas.

I sent a smiley emoji and closed up the car. When we arrived at the school, everyone was already at work, eager to beat the worst of the heat on what might be another record-breaking heatwave in Octonia.

The volunteers had already pulled up about a third of the floorboards in the front classroom, and I was glad to be able to spell them a bit, with Saul's help, when I arrived. They already looked tuckered. This was sometimes the hardest part because the board fasteners had been pressed into the joists over years. It could be tough to convince them to come loose.

I managed to get a row of boards up myself, and Saul took what was already free and got it to the truck while we organized to move as quickly as possible. The engineering students and I headed toward the back classroom and left Jamila, Rufus, Shelley, and Foster with Saul in the front. The boys were not necessarily in fighting shape, but they were strong. I figured with the three of us working we could keep pace with the older folks, especially since we had about a third of the floor rotted out.

Plus, while I didn't say this, I thought it best to keep the classmates away from the site of Ms. Agee's burial place, both for emotional and evidentiary reasons. Savannah and Santiago had checked very carefully for evidence, but in the light of day, anything might turn up.

I could hear the other crew laughing in the room as they worked, but the boys and I mostly stayed silent as we moved methodically across the room and pulled up the boards. Fortunately, things gave way more easily than they might have, and we were done removing the floor in an hour or so.

While the guys went to get some water, I scoured the earth near where Ms. Agee's skeleton had been, but I didn't see anything at all. That was both good and bad. Good that I didn't have to hide anything from everyone else. Bad, because it meant we didn't have more to go on to solve her murder.

But with the floor up, all we needed to do was lift the joists off the footers where they rested, and we would be done. Fortunately that was work best done with the forklift, so Sawyer parked his bike and climbed up with Saul. They had the joists up and loaded in short order, and when Saul pulled out with the full load of timber to drop off over by the VFW hall at the edge of town, my new friends and I took a minute to drink some water and stare at the barren hole where the school had stood.

"Seems like there should be a monument to that teacher here or something," one of the students said.

"You read my mind, young man," Rufus said and turned toward his car. He came back a moment later with a beautiful cross made from what looked like oak. Into the cross bar, he had wood burned "Hortense Agee" and on the vertical post, it read, below her name, "Beloved Teacher."

Foster picked up a hammer, and Ms. Agee's former students tapped the cross into the ground where her body had been just a few days earlier. Then, Shelley brought out a bouquet of sunflowers and placed them by the grave.

"This land belongs to my family," she said. "We'll do something more permanent soon, but for now, she will be remembered."

I pulled Sawyer against my hip, and he, for once, stood still and remained quiet. Even children know a solemn moment when they see it.

Then, we headed toward our cars. I told everyone that I planned to write about the school and Ms. Agee in my newsletter that weekend, if that was okay with them, and they all agreed it would be a fitting tribute. Foster said he and Rufus would send over a few notes about their plans for the community center for the article, and then, we pulled out from the field and went our separate ways.

As Sawyer sang some ditty he had made up about digging holes, I thought about how bittersweet these jobs always were ... about the way they gave me the privilege of getting to know people and about how hard it was to then part from those folks. Not for the first time, I gave thanks for the fact that I lived in a rural place, where I could know almost everyone well.

Sawyer and I had a bit of time to kill before Claire would be at the store since the work had gone so quickly that morning, so we took a drive out through the country to our favorite hollow. Sawyer jumped out as soon as I loosened his belt, and when he dove headfirst into the river where we'd stopped. I laughed. He had learned to swim last summer, and the river wasn't deep.

As he spent the next few minutes blazing rocks into the water around him and trying to splash me in the process, I looked up the hollow to where we'd taken down an old barn a few months earlier. The woman who owned that land had been someone I thought I'd stay in touch with, but then things had gone weird after we found a skeleton under the barn. I hadn't heard from her since, but I had the feeling I would soon. I wasn't sure why, and I didn't like the feeling.

I shook off the sense of dread and watched Sawyer play for a few more minutes before I stripped him down and wrapped him in the towel I always kept in the car for such situations.

Then, we drove on over to the store, where I forced Sawyer to do the horrible job of dressing before he jumped out to hug Claire. She wouldn't have minded, but this boy did have to learn a bit about decorum at some point.

When he did emerge from the car, though, he flew into Claire's arms, and she proceeded to spin him around and around far more times than my middle-aged body would allow. One weasel around the mulberry bush was enough to do me in, so it was good to see him laughing as she twirled and twirled him.

The rest of the morning went along as well as the first part. Claire took to helping customers with a natural acumen born both of her intelligence and her deep interest in people. She sold one woman a set of Victorian corbels because she told the customer that they looked stately, just like she did. It wasn't every woman that wanted to look *stately*, but this one did, and she purchased without a second thought.

By the time it came for Claire's lunch break, she was a studied hand at the shop, and her confidence had blossomed. When I suggested that she get lunch and then, when she came back, I'd leave her to her work, she didn't bat an eye. "Sounds good, Ms. S.," she said. "See you in an hour."

I texted Santiago and suggested a change of venue. *Feel like sorting on the porch?*

How many paper weights do you have? he replied.

One moment please, I responded as I turned to Saw and asked, "How many rocks can you bring to the porch when we get home?"

"One million," he said without hesitation.

We have one million paper weights, I texted.

Excellent.

We finalized a timeline, and I went about fidgeting with things in the store to see if I could find just one more way to highlight them well. By the time I had moved everything a single inch before moving it right back, Claire had returned from lunch, and Sawyer had actually decided he was ready to go home.

"I want pizza," he announced after we said goodbye to Claire. I sighed. "We don't have any pizza at home, but we do have bread and sauce and cheese if you want to make some."

"Okay," he said, and then promptly dozed off in the car on the ride home. Fortunately, the nap was early enough and brief enough that I thought bedtime would still go okay, and the little boost it gave him to see Santi waiting in the driveway woke him right up.

"I'm going to make bread pizza," he announced as he grabbed Santiago's hand and pulled him to the door.

"Well, okay then," Santi said as he shot me a quick wave before jogging along with Saw.

I unloaded the two totes of papers from the back and took them right to the front porch. When I went in, Beauregard had decided he was ready for his weekly outing and slipped past me out the door. He wasn't exactly the most active hunter, but when he did go out, he managed to keep our mouse and vole populations under control. I wouldn't say he earned his keep, but at least he pretended to.

The pizza making was well underway, and I took out cold cuts and cheese for Santiago and me. He grabbed the bag of chips I always kept over the fridge, and within ten minutes, we were all sitting down to our lunch. Sawyer had eschewed all baking of his pizza – "I hate the oven" – so he was eating bread with cold tomato sauce and cheese. But at least he was eating.

When we were done, I set the boys out to gather paper weights and did a quick tidy of the kitchen before checking in with Mika. It was an odd day when I didn't see her, and this looked to be one of those odd days. But she was swamped at the store in the best way, so I told her I'd catch up with her for my work day at her shop tomorrow.

Then, I went outside so Santiago and I could get started before I had to run Sawyer to his dad's for the weekend. Before we took anything out of the bins, Santi photographed everything as I had it, and I made sure to send him the photos I'd snapped of the drawers. At least we had tried to hold up evidentiary procedures, I supposed.

With that formality out of the way, I dove in. First, I sorted out all the spiral-bound books and then I made a stack of the papers. I handed Santi the books and began to organize the papers myself.

Most of them were lesson plans or really poor-quality copies of the kind of worksheets I'd seen in my own school days. But since I hadn't seen any sort of method of copying them at the school, I figured Ms. Agee must have simply used them as guides for what she wrote on the board.

As we rifled through the papers and used Sawyer's ever-growing supply of paperweights to hold down our categories and the brief notes we were each taking, we shared what we were finding. Santiago showed me Shelley's, Rufus's, and Foster's names in one gradebook. Apparently, they all had excellent penmanship.

I held up a spelling test key that featured "serendipity" as the bonus word and then a history quiz where the essay question was about Medgar Evers. This teacher was clearly dedicated to giving her students as full a range of knowledge as she could bestow.

But as fun as it was to look through her papers, we weren't finding much to give us any sense of why someone had killed her. No threatening notes. No journals to reveal her own thoughts on things. Nothing that you wouldn't expect to find in a teacher's desk, including a lewd drawing of a certain part of the male anatomy by a boy named Davey, who had been so proud as to sign his art.

I was beginning to give up hope of finding what we wanted when I came to a stack of envelopes held together with a piece of twine. I'd seen similar stacks of letters in my mother's belongings after she had died. She had kept every letter my father had ever written her from the time they met until the day she died, and she wrapped each bundle with a piece of twine just like this one. The very similarity brought tears to my eyes.

But when I flipped over the letters, I started. The writing on the front screamed angry with its wild angles and slashing lines. Each one was addressed to "Adulterer Agee." I held up the first envelope to show Santiago, and then I turned it over to open it.

Ms. Agee had used a letter opener to cleanly slice open each missive, and when I pulled the first letter out, it was clear she had cried when she read it because the paper had that wrinkly appearance that occurs when paper gets wet. I read the letter out loud to Santiago:

WOMAN,

I DON'T KNOW *who you think you are parading around this town like you are a free woman when you have a husband back home who needs you. You have no business here in Octonia, and if you know what's good for you, you'll get back to where you came from.*

THE LETTER WAS NOT SIGNED, of course, but it was hand-written, which might be something if we could find someone who might recognize the hand. I thought it looked fairly masculine to me, but I was no handwriting expert.

I passed that letter to Santiago and opened the next. Each was more of the same. Threats about what would happen to Ms. Agee if she didn't leave, some in graphic and disturbing detail. But it was the next-to-last letter that caught my attention. In it, the writer referred to Terrance Harlow and said he'd "realized his mistake" before it was too late and hoped she would, too.

"We need to talk to Terrance again," I said as I passed that letter over to Santiago.

The final letter in the stack was different from the others. The handwriting on the front was softer, more rounded, and it was addressed "To My Hateful Admirer."

I showed it to Santi, and when he gave me the go ahead, I carefully slid my finger under the edge of the flap and opened it up. Inside, there was a letter from Hortense Agee herself.

DEAR SIR,

I REALIZE *that my decision to remain at my post as the teacher of your child has left you with no end to your hatred. I can only say that I have stayed out of loyalty to the children and to my duty as a teacher.*

Your PERNICIOUS ATTACKS *on my good name have left me weary and afraid, but if I have learned anything in my life it's this: Tired and Scared are no reasons to run.*

. . .

So I will be staying, despite your threats. Please refrain from writing me further as it will do no good whatsoever.

Sincerely,
   Hortense Agee

I stared at the letter for a long moment before letting Santiago take a look.

"She knew who was threatening her," I whispered.

"Yes, she did," he said as he carefully slid the letter back in the envelope. "Now, if only we knew."

I grabbed the grade books from where he had stacked them by his feet. "We have a start," I said as I stood up to go get my laptop.

By the time I had to leave to take Sawyer to his father's house, we had begun a spreadsheet with every student's name in it. Santiago said he'd keep going while I ran Sawyer over, and when I came back, he had completed the list of names.

Fortunately, it wasn't massive, but still, searching through eighty-three names was going to take some time. I sighed as I looked at the list, and then I smiled. This was just the kind of puzzle I loved to solve.

While Santiago ordered Indian food via a delivery service from Charlottesville, I began inputting the names into a genealogy site one by one, and then as I discovered that some of the students had already died, I added another column to the spreadsheet and entered their death date. Then, I added in more columns for their parents' names, since it seemed we were probably looking for someone's father.

Then, once I had that information as complete as I could, I began to see if I could locate the living students. I didn't get far before the food arrived, but I was into the process enough to know that most of the folks still lived nearby.

While we ate, I listened as Santiago talked through how he was going to go about investigating the letters. The process included sampling enough of the handwriting to show people to see if they recognized it but keeping the exact contents of the letter and to whom it was addressed secret. "There's no use in stirring up a bunch of worry if no one can tell me who sent the letters," he said.

I finished my bite of paneer and nodded. "Agreed. Plus, from what I saw so far, some of these parents are still living. You don't want to tip them off."

"Good point," he said. "How much information can you get me on the living students?"

I shook my head. "Not that much. I can't even tell you, for sure, that they're all living, but I bet Xzanthia can help us out."

He nodded enthusiastically. "Great plan. You have time to go see her with me tomorrow? I might need your help translating her history-speak."

I grinned. "Gladly. Claire's got the shop, and all I need to do is get my newsletter out. Otherwise, I'm free all day."

He laughed. "Perfect," he said as he stood. "I love your enthusiasm. Now, can I interest you in some ice cream to fuel your research?"

I patted my belly. "I don't know. I had three samosas and that great curry." I rolled my eyes. "Who am I kidding? Of course I want ice cream."

While he cleared the plates, I dove back into my work and quickly figured out who lived nearby, or nearby enough to make a visit from the sheriff possible. By the time I finished my work and my ice cream, I had a list of nineteen names of people who had been students of Ms. Agee and who lived, as best I could tell, in or near Octonia.

"I can do an internet search and see if I can get addresses," I said as I set the laptop aside to look at my boyfriend.

"No, I can do that through my resources, but before I do, I would like to see what Xzanthia has to say about these letters and likely suspects, see if she recognizes the handwriting, too." He reached over and took my hand. "But now, I think we've done enough. Want to watch some more Bake Off?"

I grinned at him. "It's cake week," I said.

6

We didn't really watch much of Bake Off, if I'm honest. Between the kissing and then the fact that I dozed off before the showstopper, it was a quiet but fun night. And when I said good night to Santiago and made my way up to bed, I dropped off into a deep sleep that moved me into rich dreams of handsome police officers and murderous pens.

The next morning, though, I woke up refreshed despite my strange dreams, and I had an idea. I texted Santiago right away, and he gave me the go-ahead. So I sat in bed and wrote out my newsletter including a photographic sample of the handwriting we were trying to identify.

I talked about Ms. Agee, shared some quotes from her former students, and then told my readers that I was hoping to solve a little literary mystery by identifying the author of a set of letters we found in her old desk. I included the picture and then asked people to let me know if they wanted to tell me anything more about Ms. Agee or could identify the person belonging to that handwriting.

My email list had grown substantially over the past few

months, so I was now writing to about 2,000 people a week, most of them Octonia residents. Between the mystery element, the history angle, and the tie to a local person of note, I figured we might get a slew of information very quickly.

While I showered and got ready to meet Santiago at Mika's shop, I thought of all those TV scenarios with the tip lines where most of the information is bogus or useless, and I hoped that wouldn't be the case with my email list. But when I got out, I had only one message, and it was from Rufus. "Thank you for paying tribute to her so well," it said. And that was all.

I quelled my disappointment by reminding myself that it was Saturday morning and not everyone was on their computers first thing on the weekend, and then I packed up the totes with the papers we needed and drove to town for the day.

While I helped Mika straighten the store and put out a few of our "shelf enhancers" from the back room, I filled her in on the latest. She listened intently and said, "You know that whoever wrote those letters is going to want to get them from you, don't you?"

I stopped fluffing the eyelash yarn in the basket in front of me and said, "Why didn't I think of that?" Suddenly, I was very nervous about the email I'd just sent. If someone thought I knew who they were and knew I had those letters, I could be in danger. Sawyer could be in danger.

Mika pulled me to her and gave me a hug. "Don't worry, Paisley. I'm just thinking the worst. Ignore me."

I shook my head. "No, you're right." I took the packet of letters out of my bag. "I need to get these to Santiago right away."

Just then, the bell over Mika's door rang and Santi walked in.

"Oh thank goodness," I said. "I may be in danger." I held up the letters. "I think I made a mistake."

He smiled but then grew serious, "You mean in your email

this morning?" He took the letters from my hand. "You were just trying to ask questions. You couldn't have known." He gave me a quick hug. "But think about it this way. We can identify everyone on your list, so if they come after you from there, we can determine who they are."

"Some comfort," Mika said with a roll of her eyes. "It's like the way a woman has to be attacked by a stalker before anything can be done about it." She huffed and walked off toward the back of the store.

I watched her for a minute and then followed behind. "What's going on?" I asked. "Are you okay?"

She sighed. "Sorry," she said to Santi over my shoulder. "I know that's not what you intended, but I just get so frustrated by all these ways people are allowed to do awful things and it feels like people, women in particular, are left vulnerable."

Mika and I had seen that exact thing play out with women we knew again and again. It made us scared and worried, and honestly, I felt a little powerless, even now. But Mika's reaction seemed a little intense for the moment. "Did something happen?"

She shook her head. "No, just watched that show *Maid*." She put her hands up above her head and then dropped them. "Stirred some stuff up for me."

I had purposefully not watched the program because I was worried about that very thing for myself. "You okay?" I asked.

"I am, but Santi, you have to be able to protect Paisley, right? I mean, she should be able to ask some historical questions without fearing for her life, shouldn't she?" Mika's eyes were wide, and I thought she might cry.

Santiago took a deep breath. "I'm not going to let anything happen to her, Mika. And you're right. She should be able to ask questions without fear of being in danger. Unfortunately, not everyone thinks that way." He took out his phone. "I'll stay

here today, work from the store, and then take a break to visit
Ms. Nicholas, if that's okay with you?"

Mika visibly relaxed. "Yes, please. And thank you."

I smiled. "Yes, thank you," I said as he turned and called the
station to let them know where he was. "I love you," I said to my
best friend.

"I love you, too, and sorry. I just get so worried about you
sometimes." She hugged me.

I smiled. "And I get worried about you, too. How are things
with Dom?" Mika had started dating one of Santiago's good
friends a few months ago, and things had been a bit rocky,
mostly because they both had to get their feet under them after
hard break-ups in the past.

"Actually, they're pretty good. We're going out tomorrow."
She sighed. "I just wish we could see each other more. Between
the store and his business and his daughter, there just isn't
enough time."

I nodded and thought about how Dom also lived down in
town, which wasn't that far, but when you were as busy as these
two, even forty-five minutes apart made things more difficult. "I
hear that. Glad you get to see him tomorrow. That might make
you feel better, too."

She smiled and blushed a little. "It always does." She
turned and faced the front of the store. "You'd better get to
researching, and I have a crocheted cowl for your shop that I
need to finish."

I smiled and headed to the cozy corner and took out my
laptop. I could certainly work more efficiently from home, but
there was just something about being with my best friend in
her space that made me feel good and relaxed, even on a busy
day. And with Santiago here, I couldn't imagine a better
workspace.

When he joined me, I smiled. "Thanks for this. I love that
you're here, and I know it helps Mika today."

"It's not exactly a hardship to have to work with you all day, now is it?" He grinned. "And Savannah is going to do the legwork of showing around the handwriting sample to see if anyone recognizes it. Your email, though, may make that easier." He reached over and squeezed my hand.

"Or harder, right?" I sighed. "Sometimes my desire to know gets ahead of my better judgment."

He shook his head. "In this case, the only real problem is that, as Mika said, you made yourself a sort of target." He held up the letters. "But now that I have these, you can honestly say they've been turned over to the police and maybe alleviate a bit of the risk."

"Speaking of which," I said as I opened my laptop to see that I had four responses to my email from the morning. Two of the notes were lovely reminiscences of Ms. Agee from her former students, but the other two were more directly about the handwriting. The first from a woman who said she had gone to the school herself and said the writing looked familiar to her, but she wasn't sure why. She told me she'd think on it and get back to me if she remembered anything more.

The second response was more helpful if more cryptic. "Check out the Stone Store," it said. "Look at the countertop." The email wasn't signed, and the person had masked their name in the "From" line. I knew that Santiago could easily find the owner, but at this point, I didn't know if we needed to do that.

I spun my laptop around and showed him the message. He looked at the screen and then up at me. "The Stone Store? Do you know what that means? A store that sells stone? Like a landscaper or home supply place?"

I shrugged. "I don't know, but I know who would." I closed my laptop and told Mika we'd be back shortly. Then, Santiago walked up the street to the Historical Society.

Ms. Nicholas was not only a treasure trove of historical

information, but her family had been in Octonia for generations. Mine had, too, but like most places in the South, Octonia was still affected by the ongoing legacy of Jim Crow, and white people like me didn't always know much about black spaces. We'd never needed to – but black folks needed to understand white places really well. So Ms. Nicholas knew far more than I did, even about our hometown.

I had forwarded her the email, and when we arrived, she was waiting with a folder in front of her on the long table. "This is the Stone Store," she said pointing at a black and white photograph of a small stone building that I recognized from a nearby intersection. I must have passed it a million times in my life.

"I know that place," Santiago said. "I didn't realize it had ever been a store though."

"Had been a store?" Ms. Nicholas says. "Still is a store, sir. Best convenience store in town, and if anyone tells you that somewhere else makes the best fried chicken in the state, they are lying."

"Wait? What?! It's still an operational store?" I stared at her a minute. "I don't see lots of cars there or anything."

"Why would there be cars when most folks who shop there can walk over, Paisley?" She shook her head a little. "Stone Park is right behind there."

I nodded. I knew the little neighborhood of small 1920s homes. Simple one-story buildings that looked alike. I'd always wondered about its history but hadn't gotten around to asking. "Tell me about Stone Park?"

She gestured for us to sit down and then passed Santiago the folder of newspaper clippings. "The store was built by the Stone family to serve that community. The fact that it is built from stone is just a matter of convenience. They used the fieldstones from the place they cleared to construct our houses to build the store."

"*Our* houses?" I asked.

"Yes, Paisley. "I live in Stone Park. Have all my life. It was my parents' house and my grandparents' before them." She studied my face. "It's the only wealth my family ever had, and we worked hard to keep it."

I swallowed hard. I was still learning to understand the way people of color had been held back, and the more I learned, the more I marveled at how resilient people were. "I see. And the Stone family built the neighborhood?"

She smiled. "In a way. They had the land, and they sold plats to lots of black families in the early twentieth century so that we could have homes. Mr. Jeremiah Stone worked and saved his whole life to buy that twenty acres, and his descendants still live there today, still run the store, too, in fact."

"So the Stones from the school . . ." Santiago asked.

"Same folks, just the next generation. They helped fund the school and put up the teacher, like we discussed." She pointed to the article Santiago held in his hands. "That will give you the gist of the story."

I leaned over and read the article. It described how Humphrey and Minerva Stone had spearheaded the campaign to raise funds for the Rosenwald School. They'd quickly raised the money from their own community, but it had taken them two years to get the county to agree to chip in. Once they did, Rosenwald provided his portion, and the school was built. "To much pride in the community," the article said.

"They were real community organizers," I said. "And Shelley O'Hara?"

"Their daughter."

"Right, she said Ms. Agee had lived in her house, so that makes sense." I nodded. "So what do you make of that email then?"

Ms. Nicholas shrugged. "I don't make much of it yet, but feel like taking a ride. I know a place with great fried chicken."

"I'll drive," Ms. Nicholas said as we walked outside, and she led us to a beautiful, white BMW sedan. "Get in and buckle up."

I laughed, thinking she was just being playful, but when she squealed out of the driveway onto Main Street, I was glad I'd gotten in the back. If this was going to be a dangerous ride, I thought having the sheriff in the front seat might temper her speed.

Fortunately, she was a very safe if very fast driver, and by the time we had driven the half mile or so out of town, I understood why. That car had power, and it was so smooth. I was already scheming how to get a road trip scheduled with Ms. Nicholas, Mika, and me – in her car of course.

When she parked beside in the gravel parking lot of the store, I carefully opened the door and stepped out. I didn't want to ding the door on that beautiful vehicle. She led us in through the glass door on the side of the building, and when we got inside, I grinned.

It felt like we had stepped back in time fifty years. The floors were broad, wooden boards, and the shelves were wooden, too. A small deli sat at the back with modern cooking equipment but also a vintage hood that looked like those I'd seen in the diners I loved so much.

"Let me order for us, and I'll be right back. Why don't you all take a look around?" Ms. Nicholas winked at us, and we did as we were told.

The shelves were stocked with the usual convenience store fare, everything from candy bars to toilet paper to cigarettes and soda. The stock was tidy and clean, and I quickly grabbed up two candy bars – a Baby Ruth for me and a Hershey's bar for Sawyer, our favorites.

As we milled around and looked at the more obscure things that edged the shop, a selection of beautiful, hand-made scarves, a small section of handmade wooden toys, a wonderful assortment of what seemed to be hand-poured candles, I tried to take note of the people in the store. It was the middle of the afternoon, so there weren't many of us milling about. But everyone else in the shop, including the two employees, were black.

A year or so ago, being the minority in a place might have felt disconcerting to me, but since I'd been spending more and more time with Santiago's Latinx family and attending Bethel Church, where I was the only white member, I'd grown used to that situation and even liked it. I always felt welcome and safe, even if I also sometimes felt a bit out of place.

At the moment, I felt completely comfortable and was glad to know this place existed. I picked up the cards of the candle maker and toymaker and made a note in my phone to contact them to see if they wanted to sell some of their wares at my shop. The scarves were gorgeous, too, but I didn't want to give Mika any competition for her sales.

When I saw Ms. Nicholas walking our way, we met her by the counter, and as I paid for my items, she introduced me to the woman behind the counter, Benita. "Benita, Paisley here received a strange note today in response to her history news-letter. The writer suggested she look at the counter here in your store. Any ideas?"

Benita grinned. "Sure do. Look right here." She moved a few things off the side of the counter and tapped one purple nail on the wood. "Been here for years. Only the old-timers ask to see it now, for the most part, but it's a lot of history right here."

I stepped around the counter and stared down. There, in the wood, were hundreds of signatures. "It's like an autograph book," Ms. Nicholas said from behind me.

"Exactly. Folks have been signing it since the store opened. Mostly they come on special days. Weddings, birthdays and such. But sometimes people just sign it because they remember right then." Benita pointed at one signature. "This is my daddy's signature, right here. Signed it the day I was born." She smiled down at her father's handwriting. "Someday, maybe we'll frame it and put it up on the wall, but not yet. Still got some folks that want to add to it."

I looked up from the board into Benita's face. "Someone suggested I might recognize some handwriting from here, but with so many signatures, I could stare at this all day and probably not find what the person meant."

"You got a sample of what you're looking for?" she asked.

Santiago took his phone out and showed her an image he'd snapped of one of the letters. "Sure thing," he said.

Benita's eyes scanned the screen, and a frown creased her forehead. "Well, that's not hard at all, but do you mind me asking what this is about?"

I looked at Santiago and then over at Ms. Nicholas, who also nodded. "We found Ms. Agee's body over at the school," I said. If Benita knew this community as well as she seemed to, then I didn't need to give her more details for her to be able to put things together.

She sat back on the stool behind her. "Alright then. Mama and Daddy talk about Ms. Agee all the time still. She was a good woman. A good teacher," she whispered.

"That's what everyone says," I replied quietly. "We just want to find out what happened to her."

Benita stared at the counter with the all the signatures for a long moment, and then she looked up at me. "That's Humphrey Stone's handwriting," she said before she stood and pointed to the signature that was top and center on the board.

Clear as day, the board read, "Humphrey Stone" in a hand that looked very similar to the one that had written the threatening letters to Ms. Agee. I didn't doubt Benita's identification, but I needed to know more. "How are you sure?"

She looked up at me, and it took a second for her eyes to

focus. "Oh, right. Look at the T. He always crossed it with an S." She looked down and put her finger on the T. "Told me once it was because he always wanted to remember the strength of his name."

I looked from the counter to the image of Santiago's phone and back. Sure enough, the cross hatch on the T was definitely in the shape of an S, and each mark was identical on both pieces of writing. Even when it wasn't in his name, Stone had crossed his Ts with that S. It was as distinctive a marker as I expected we'd ever find.

Santiago slipped his phone in his pocket and then held out his hand to Benita. "Thank you. Now, I need to ask you to keep this to yourself, or talk about it only with Ms. Nicholas. You can understand why, right?"

Benita nodded. "I can, and I won't say a thing. I don't know exactly what you're trying to figure out or where you got Mr. Stone's handwriting, but I've no desire to get mucked up in this stuff. You have my word."

"Thank you," Santiago said. "Now, where do we eat this amazing fried chicken that I can smell?"

WHEN THE THREE of us took our seats on a worn picnic table under a tree behind the building, I couldn't resist peeling a strip of the crispy skin off my chicken leg and savoring the greasy goodness as I ate. "This is the best chicken I've ever had," I said as I took my second bite.

"I told you," Ms. Nicholas said as she managed to handle her huge breast with her usual amount of poise and grace. "Best in the state."

"Maybe in the country," Santiago said with his mouth full. "The mac and cheese is pretty killer, too."

I tried not to talk with my mouth full, but I nodded and moaned enthusiastically in agreement as I ate my own serving

of macaroni and cheese, savoring the crusty bits from the edge
of the pan.

For a few minutes, we all enjoyed our food, but once we'd
cleared our plates of chicken, mac and cheese, and the best
green beans I'd ever tasted, the looming subject of the fact that
Mr. Stone, Shelley's father, had written those threatening letters
to Ms. Agee had to be addressed. I took the first stab at the
issue. "There must be something we're not seeing, right? I
mean he had the woman living in his home."

Santiago sighed. "I've been thinking about that. What if
there was something, um, inappropriate going on between Mr.
Stone and Ms. Agee." He blushed a little as he finished his
statement and looked tentatively at Ms. Nicholas.

"He was a good man, but even good people make mistakes. I
don't think we can rule that out," she said. "But I think we'd be
wise to keep that hypothesis amongst ourselves." She gave each
of us a pointed look.

I swallowed hard. "Agreed. We're not going to get much
cooperation if we sully the name of a hometown hero." I looked
at Santiago. "So where do we go from here, Sheriff Shifflett?"

"Well, for the sake of dotting our Is and crossing our Ts," he
smiled and looked at each of us, "I hope Savannah is able to get
confirmation of the handwriting's originator. I'm sure Benita is
right, but we need solid evidence. I'm just not sure a judge will
think a signature on a board is enough."

"Makes sense," I said as I wiped my greasy fingers on my
napkin for the third time. "But how do we figure out what was
going on with Mr. Stone and Ms. Agee without implicating
him?"

"We investigate Ms. Agee," Ms. Nicholas said with a frown.
"I don't like to be digging into the life of a woman who was
murdered, but something tells me our answers will be easier to
find there than in digging around with the local folks."

I sat staring at my hands for a few minutes, trying to think of another option, one that didn't mean we had to delve into the life of a dead woman, a murdered woman, but I couldn't come up with anything. The truth was that Octonia was a small place where everyone knew everyone else's business. If we started asking around about Mr. Stone or the letters in any detail, people would connect the dots and either cover things up – we'd had that happen before – or muddy the waters so much that we wouldn't be able to tell truth from fiction. Ms. Nicholas was right. "So we're taking a trip to Fluvanna?" I asked.

Santiago stood up, cleared the table, and said, "This afternoon work for you?"

I let him help me to my feet. "It does, but only if we can make it a group trip." I looked at Ms. Nicholas. "You in?"

"Of course, I'm in. Just let me go back and change into my clue-hunting shoes." She then kicked a leg up onto the table with the flare of the Rockettes and showed us her stiletto heels. "These boots are made for walking . . . but not in fields." She laughed and led the way to her car.

BY THE TIME we got back to Mika's shop, she had brought in her assistant, Mrs. Stephenson, and she joined me in the back of Ms. Nicholas's car. I leaned over and whispered, "Hold on," but she didn't need the warning.

As soon as Ms. Nicholas gunned the engine, Mika let out a whoop and opened her window to let the wind blow through her hair. Clearly, she was better with speedy cars than I was.

But by the time we got to Fluvanna about an hour later, I was loving the speed and power of the car. In fact, the joy of riding in it made me forget the purpose of our trip almost entirely as I let the rumble of the engine ease some of the tension in my back.

Most of that tension returned, however, as soon as we

stepped foot outside the tiny church where Ms. Nicholas had parked. She had reached out to a local historian who was the secretary of this church, and the woman had agreed to meet us with all the records the church had about the Agee family, who had been members of the church for over a hundred and fifty years.

What Ms. Nicholas neglected to mention, perhaps because she didn't know but I suspect more because she knew it would freak me out, was that Ms. Agee's great-niece, Angelia, was going to be meeting us at the church, too.

So when a woman about my age and a wonderful older woman with a walker came out of the side door to the church, I was a little surprised, but not so much that I forgot my manners. I shook the hands of both women and then followed them inside, where they had set up a wonderful spread of snacks, drinks, and history on one of the fellowship hall tables. Ms. Nicholas made introductions between us and Angelia and Mrs. Alva Key, the historian.

"I'm not sure what Ms. Nicholas has told you all," Santiago began once we were all seated with iced tea and shortbread, "but would you like me to tell you why we're here?"

Mrs. Key said, "Yes sir, we would. Xzanthia here has told us some things, but it always helps to have things repeated. Right, Angelia?"

The younger woman smiled. "Yes, ma'am." She looked over at me and winked as if to say, "Repetition is sometimes necessary with age."

I smiled and sat back to let Santi fill them in. Both women nodded along, frowned in the appropriate places, and took some notes. In short, they acted just as they should when hearing about a woman, a relative even, who was murdered. But something about their reaction just wasn't sitting right with me, and I couldn't figure out why.

Finally, with all the details we knew, except the name

Humphrey Stone, disclosed, Ms. Nicholas sat back, folded her hands in her lap, and waited. I followed suit because, after all, these were her friends and this was her show.

It didn't take long before the reason for my discomfort became clear. Angelia said, "You're sure it was my great-aunt Hortense?"

Santiago looked at me and then over at Ms. Nicholas. "Fairly sure. Why?"

"Because my Aunt Hortense lived to be ninety-four years old and lived right next door here to the church until the day she died." The woman made her statement so matter-of-factly that I had no doubt she was telling the truth.

Ms. Nicholas sat forward and calmly said, "So you are saying that the woman whose body was found under the school by my home was not Hortense Agee?"

Both Ms. Key and Angelia shook their heads. "At least she wasn't the Hortense Agee we knew. Maybe it was a woman with the same name?" Ms. Key suggested.

I put my hands on top of my head and looked up at the ceiling. "I guess that's possible, but I just don't think it's likely. After all, the Hortense Agee who taught in Octonia said she was from Fluvanna – from here in fact. She told her students she had ties to this church."

Angelia and Ms. Key exchanged a glance and then said, "The only thing we can think is that someone stole her identity and was making a living off her name and credentials."

"So your Aunt Hortense was a teacher?" Santiago said as he drew his notebook from his breast pocket.

"Yes, she attended Hampton and then came back here to teach in the school across the road for forty-five years," Angelia said. "She taught most of the older people in our community."

"Including me," Ms. Key added. "Best teacher I ever had. I followed in her footsteps in fact. Went to Virginia State and became a teacher, too."

"And you were the best teacher I ever had," Angelia said as she leaned over and hugged Ms. Key before turning back to us. "But you see, I think you have the wrong person. My great-aunt lived a long life, and aside from the years she was at college, she never lived anywhere else."

I looked at Ms. Nicholas, and for once, I saw a bit of strain on her face. She took a deep breath, though, and then said, "This may be a very long shot, but did your aunt leave any papers behind."

Ms. Key reached behind her and picked up a translucent tote. "We must believe in the same long shots, Xzanthia," she said as she set the tote on the table. "With Angelia's permission, I'm loaning you all the papers her aunt left behind. We're in the process of cataloging them to donate to the historical society here, so you'll also find our partial finding aid right on top."

Ms. Nicholas opened the lid of the tote and smiled. "I will take the best care of them," she said.

"I have no doubt, and I do hope they help you solve this murder," Ms. Key said as she looked at the sheriff. "You'll let us know what you find out?"

"Yes, please," Angelia added. "It doesn't sound like this woman harmed my aunt's reputation , but all the same, I'd like to understand why she did what she did – and what happened to her."

"Absolutely," I said after Santiago nodded. "And if you don't mind, I'd like to profile your aunt in my small newsletter when we figure out this story, give her recognition as who she was instead of as the person who used her name."

Angelia smiled. "That would be lovely. Thank you."

I gave both women a hug before we left, and I tried to keep my smile in place as Ms. Nicholas pulled out. But I didn't feel like smiling even a little bit. We now had three mysteries to solve, and I had no idea where to look for answers next.

7

The drive back to Octonia was even quieter than the one down, and only when we headed west toward home, did Mika say. "I'm actually glad that it was the fact that Ms. Agee had lived a long life that the women had to tell us. I was getting a squirrely sense from them, and I didn't want to dislike them or think ill of them."

Ms. Nicholas laughed. "Squirrely is right. I've known Alva Key for almost thirty years, and I'd never seen her be so cagey. Now, I know why. She wanted to be sure she understood what we knew before she told us the truth. Wise woman, she is."

I sighed. "Yeah, if she knew the whole story about the woman I will now call Ms. Doe, then she didn't give us room to argue. She and Angelia saved us a lot of time and energy."

The silence sat heavy in the car for a few moments, but then the text chime on Santiago's phone went off. "It's confirmed. The handwriting definitely belonged to Humphrey Stone. Two other people identified his Ts from the sample Savannah showed," he said. "I don't know what that means though. Was he threatening a woman he really thought to be

Ms. Agee, or did he figure out she wasn't who she said she was and threatened her for that reason?"

I rubbed my fingers into my eyes. "I have no idea, but I could use some food and beer to think through all of this. Burgers and beer at my house?"

Mika and Santiago agreed immediately, but when Ms. Nicholas paused, I thought she was going to offer a kind but clear reason for not coming. Instead, she said, "Sounds perfect. I'll bring the real Ms. Agee's papers, but first I need to go home and change. I'll bring a six-pack of my favorite beer, too."

I laughed. "You drink beer?"

"Like a fish," she said as she pulled up in front of Mika's shop. "See you at your place in thirty?"

"Perfect," I said. "Want to come along to the shop and check in?" I looked from Santi to Mika.

"Of course, I do, and besides, we're not leaving you alone. That's what we agreed," Santiago said.

Mika nodded vehemently, and I smiled. "Alright, should only take a minute."

We hopped into my car and headed out of town to Saul's lot. The lights were still on in the shed, and I could see Claire moving about. When I stepped in, she grinned at me. "I was just about to text you."

"Oh yeah?" I said as my eyes scanned the space and saw everything looked great, even a bit emptier.

"Yep. I just sold that lot of barnwood and the old plow." She beamed with delight and pride.

I stepped forward and gave her a hug. "Wow. Those are big sales. How do you feel about the price you got?"

Her smile grew even wider. "Well, since I got ten percent more than you asked on the wood and your full asking price on the plow, I feel pretty good."

This time, I was beaming. "You are a rock star," I said and pulled her into a chair to hear the whole story about her negotiation with the young couple building their dream cabin up in the woods above town and how they wanted everything to be locally sourced and reclaimed if possible. "The clincher, though, was when they said they wanted to support local businesses, especially those owned by women."

"Ooh, you're a savvy business woman for sure, Claire," I said and gave her another quick hug.

While we'd talked, Santi had stepped outside to take care of some emails and calls, and Mika had adjusted the placement of her yarn pieces to give them a fresh look.

"Oh, and I sold three scarves, a cowl, and that gorgeous cable-knit sweater," Claire said as she walked toward Mika. "That same woman who bought the boards bought the sweater when I told her you were a woman who ran her own business, too."

"Ooh, girl, you have got this sales thing down," Mika said as she gave Claire a high five.

I glanced around again and told Claire the shop looked great and that we could close up now. I had seen Saul's truck by his office, so I knew he'd stayed on site, as we'd agreed, to keep an eye on Claire, but I also knew he'd want to get home and relax. And I wasn't about to leave Claire here alone.

We quickly did the closing chores and then locked up the shed, made sure the chains were around the things that might walk off, and then loaded into our cars. I gave a long beep as we left to let Saul know we were gone, and I saw him step to the door of his office and wave before turning out the lights.

CLAIRE TURNED LEFT to go back to town, and we made the right to go to my house. I'd thought about pulling into the gas station up the road to get another six-pack, but then I remembered the bottle of whiskey that Mika and I had bought to try some fancy, summer drink. Beer and whiskey seemed about right for tonight.

The drive home was short, and we pulled in just as Ms. Nicholas was parking her car. I could see Beauregard on the kitchen table at the window, and he looked quite grumpy, even more so than usual. He must have run out of kibble and felt it necessary to let me know he might have starved had I not come home immediately.

I unlocked the door and slipped inside, glad to feel the air conditioner had kept the house moderately cool, even though I ran it a bit warmer than usual when I wasn't home to keep the bill down. Another reason Beau might be crochety – he had a precise temperature preference, and this was not it.

Mika tried to give the cat a pet, but his low growl sent her backwards with a roll of her eyes. So she and I set to putting out the food while Santi got the drinks ready and Ms. Nicholas approached Beau with a slow, steady smile and a low stream of words that had him purring before she even put a hand on him.

"You are the cat whisperer," I said as I looked at the two of them and put out the burgers.

"What is this handsome fellow's name?" she asked.

Mika rolled her eyes again. "Don't feed his ego. It's already sucking all the oxygen out of the room."

I smiled. "That is Beauregard."

"What an appropriately distinguished name for such a regal fellow." Ms. Nicholas leaned closer and whispered loudly enough for us to hear. "I bet they call you Beau, and you hate it, don't you?"

Beau turned his chin up to her and rubbed firmly against her outstretched hand in affirmation. This time I rolled my eyes. "Alright, then, I'll try to remember to call you by your full name, Your Highness," I said.

His purr grew noticeably louder, and we all laughed. Ms. Nicholas gave him one last stroke and then gently set him on the floor before asking if she could give him some dinner while we ate. I pointed her to the food and made a mental note to ask her to cat sit the next time I needed someone to stay with my persnickety kitty.

We enjoyed the burgers and the beer, and after dinner, Santiago poured us each a finger of whiskey before going out to Ms. Nicholas's car and getting the tote of papers. Then, we took our drinks and our questions into the living room and got to work.

Mika and Ms. Nicholas reviewed the partial finding aid while Santiago and I removed the papers in their tidy bundles and files and arranged them around the room. Then Ms. Nicholas used sticky notes to mark the piles that seemed most useful to our query before settling herself in the corner chair to sort the small stack of heretofore unorganized papers. "It's the least I can do since they loaned us the files," she said as she attached the finding aid to her clipboard and began to work.

I selected a stack of letters that Ms. Nicholas had marked and settled onto the couch to read while Santiago picked up what looked like lessons plans. Mika took another stack of letters, and we all began to read.

It was a quiet hour while we each carefully and methodically worked through our chosen piles, and when no one had a great find in that first jag, Santi refilled our glasses and distributed a second set of documents to each of us.

This time, I was working with a set of letters that was unusual because a quick scan through the pile told me it contained both letters from and to Ms. Agee. I stared at the return address on the second letter and took a deep breath: Octonia. No name, but a rural route with the Octonia town address and zip code.

I started to tell everyone what I'd found but decided not to get folks' hopes up if it wasn't anything significant. I also decided to read the letters in the order that they were stacked because, I presumed, Angelia and Ms. Key had organized them that way for a reason. I was right. The first letter was from Ms. Agee to someone named Ethel and it was giving her advice about how to set up her classroom for her first day.

I smiled at the directions about separating the boys from each other whenever possible and about making sure her desk was located where she could see the door at all times, but beyond some sage wisdom about classroom management, I didn't see anything of use.

The second letter, dated four days later, was from Ethel Orlan and thanked Ms. Agee for the advice, which Ethel said she had taken in full. Then she asked for her wisdom about how to manage the gap in knowledge between the children in her class. "Some have had the benefit of parents who could read and write and, thus, taught them, but not all have been so fortunate." Ethel wanted to know how Ms. Agee might help all the children excel without shaming the ones who had further to go in their education.

The letters were such a tender and informative exchange of information and support from a more experienced teacher to a new one, and I savored each one because it showed me how much both of these women cared about their students and their profession. But I wasn't really finding anything that would help us figure out who Ms. Doe was.

From the looks on everyone else's faces, they were having the same results, but we kept going. Even Beauregard seemed diligent from his perch on top of Ms. Nicholas's chair. He kept a careful eye on each piece of paper she read and watched her pen closely as she made notes. I thought about warning her that he had a tendency to leap at pens as toys while they were in use, but something about his deference to Ms. Nicholas made me think she was probably safe from a swat.

I was about to open the last letter from Ms. Orlan to Ms. Agee when I noticed something on the outside of the envelope.

There on the back of the envelope, someone had written, very lightly with a pencil, "From Hortense Agee." I flipped the envelope back over, and it was definitely labeled *to* Hortense Agee, but when I reread the back, someone had also implied it was from her, too.

While holding my breath, I opened the final letter and hoped. The opening line read, "Someone has found out our ruse. I have been discovered."

I let out a long whistle and asked everyone to listen to what I'd found. I explained about the exchange of letters between teachers, told them what was written on the back of this letter, and began to read:

DEAREST MS. AGEE,

SOMEONE HAS COME upon our ruse. I have been discovered. I do not yet know how, but it is clear I must move along for my safety, and perhaps for yours, too. I am sending you all our letters because I cannot bear to destroy them, but I also cannot risk they will be found.

YOU HAVE BEEN SO KIND to me these past years, and I have so valued our friendship as well as your generosity to loan me your credentials and experience. I can only hope that someday, when it is safe for me to return, I may repay you with my full gratitude.

I WILL NOT NOTE MORE of my intentions but simply hope to set any fears you have to rest by saying I have assistance and support and will not be alone as I make my next journey.

. . .

WITH DEEPEST GRATITUDE,

ETHEL

I SET the letter in my lap and stared at it for a minute before looking up when Ms. Nicholas said, "Well good Lord almighty, she was hiding."

"Wow. Like her own form of witness protection or something," Mika said.

I sighed. "And someone found out." I held up the paper. "She didn't get away."

The silence in the room grew heavy, and I carefully folded the letter back into its envelope after Santiago took a photo of it for evidence.

"No more letters after that?" Santiago asked. "No response from Ms. Agee?"

I shook my head. "Not in this stack." I looked over at Ms. Nicholas.

"Not here either." She sighed. "That seems logical, though, doesn't it? She wouldn't have wanted to further risk exposing her."

"Yes, that does make sense," Mika said as she stood up and began pacing around the middle of the room. "But the letters to Ethel are addressed to her, right? With her name?"

I held up the stack with the first letter to Ethel on top. "Yep. Right here." I wasn't sure what my friend was thinking through, but I knew better than to interrupt.

"What's the address?" She asked.

I read off the rural route number, and Ms. Nicholas shot to her feet. "That's the old number for Stone Park Loop. She was living in my neighborhood."

Then, Mika said, "So Humphrey Stone knew." There wasn't a hint of a question in her voice.

I groaned. "The letters were going to his house, and he had to have seen them." I could feel pieces sliding into place, but still something wasn't fitting quite right. "But if using Ethel's real name was dangerous, why did Ms. Agee do that?"

"She must not have thought it was dangerous," Santi said as he leaned forward. "I think we need to reconsider even more than we thought."

"Like maybe Humphrey Stone was in on the ruse?" Mika said quietly.

"Exactly," Santiago said.

WE SPENT the next hour or so talking through the possibilities of things while we double-checked to be sure there wasn't anything more of note for our situation in Ms. Agee's papers. Nothing more came up, but while we continued to talk, Ms. Nicholas dictated her additions to the finding aid to me, and I typed them up and then printed out a sheet to add to the box and then slid the file onto a flash drive for Ms. Nicholas to give to Ms. Key as a bit of thanks.

By the time we had regathered the papers, cleaned up our glasses, and sat back down at the table – with tea this time – we had a working theory.

Mika reiterated it for all of us one last time, just to be sure we had the details sorted between us. "So Ms. Orlan was hiding from someone, and somehow, Ms. Agee became a part of her disguise, lending her name and teaching credential to the young woman. "

"Right," I said.

"And Mr. Stone knew about the situation, too, and agreed to hide Ms. Orlan in his home as well as provide cover for her teacher story," Mika continued.

"Yes, that seems most feasible," Ms. Nicholas said.

"So what we need to know," Mika said as she looked at Santiago, "is why Ms. Orlan was in hiding?"

"And how Ms. Agee and Mr. Stone came to know that she needed help," Santi added. "That might give us a good sense of why she was hiding and who killed her."

All of us sat quietly for a few minutes until Santiago said, "I think our best bet is to talk to Shelley. She might know more than she realizes she does."

Ms. Nicholas nodded. "Agreed, and the same might be true for Alva and Angelia. I'll go down and see them at their church in the morning. They always do big lunches after the service, so we can talk then."

"And I'll call on Shelley in the morning, see what she might know," Santiago said.

I looked at Mika. "You have a big date, right?"

Mika blushed. "Yes, Dom and I are going up on the parkway to escape the heat."

I winked at her. "I bet it won't be all cool up there."

"You are terrible, Paisley Sutton," she said, but her smile grew wider. "What are you going to do with your day?"

"Well, Claire is covering the shop in the morning so I can go to church, so I'll do that and then see what Mary might know at lunch." My friend knew almost as much as Ms. Nicholas, but unlike the stately director of the historical society, she also delved into the sketchier parts of our community in her work as a nurse. She might just have something enlightening to share.

"Well, we all have our marching orders," Santiago said. "We best get some good sleep. Especially you, ma'am. You've got to deal with Dom for a full day."

I grabbed my keys and wallet and headed for the door. "I'll give you a ride into town," I said.

"You'll do no such thing," Ms. Nicholas said as she took my keys and blue leather wallet from my hands. "I'm going that way, and you are going to stay here and relax with another glass of whiskey." She poured me another finger of the drink and pointed to the couch. "Now, sew."

"Yes, ma'am," I said as I moved instinctively toward my sofa.

"Your job, Sir Beauregard, is to make sure your mistress relaxes tonight. Are we clear?" Ms. Nicholas said.

With a flick of his tail, Beauregard walked to the couch, jumped up on the arm, and watched me until I sat down beside him. He then leaped over my lap and curled up beside me with one paw on my thigh nearest him. I could see the tips of his claws at the ready.

"Your sentry is in place," I said with a laugh. "Be safe, all of you, okay?"

"We will," Mika said as she slipped her arm through Ms. Nicholas's. "You're staying here, right?" She looked at Santiago.

"Already put my duffel bag in Sawyer's room," Santi said.

I raised an eyebrow. "Really?"

"Yep, remember, you're not to be left alone, not with the person who wrote that email out and about." He waved to the two women as they left, and then he carefully sat down on the other side of Beau. "You don't mind do you?" he said with a wink.

"Not even a little bit," I said as I picked up my sewing frame and moved to the next tree in my current project, a bushy thing that had to be a sugar maple. The bright red-orange thread felt lifegiving on a day that had been thoroughly confusing and not just a little bit disconcerting.

THE NEXT MORNING, after a very deep sleep brought on by more whiskey than I've ever consumed in my life, I woke up to two sounds – the purring of a very contented cat on my pillow and the sizzling of bacon. Unfortunately, these two sounds gave me conflicting motivations, so I found a compromise by staying in bed a few minutes more to cuddle Beau and then carrying him downstairs like a baby to find our bacon.

Santiago had already showered and was dressed in his uniform, a clear sign that he was taking his intended visit with Shelley very seriously. He looked and smelled amazing, and I gave him a deep hug and then came back for a long kiss as soon as I had deposited Beau on a blanket on the couch and brushed my teeth.

The bacon was cooked to perfection – a combination of crispy and chewy – and the scrambled eggs with chives and cheese that he had made to go with the bacon were amazing. Long ago, he and I had established that this idea of bacon as a side dish was backwards, so we always plated the bacon as the main course and then let folks add the sides, like eggs or pancakes, as they wished. It was our idea of a fun appreciation of this best of foods.

Today, though, we weren't too jovial as we ate. We talked through our plans for the day and tried to enjoy the bright light of a summer morning by taking a quick walk outside. But the day was already muggy, and the weight of our work for the day was heavy, too. So I went in and took a shower before he dropped me off at church and made me promise to stay at Mary's until he came back to pick me up.

When I walked into the sanctuary, I let out a long hard breath of release and forced my mind to be here, in this space, with these lovely people. Mary greeted me with a hug at our pew, and I slid past her to take my usual seat, where I could get a good view of the organist as his hands flew up and down the keys.

This morning, his prelude was "Come Thou Fount of Every Blessing," and I found the remaining strain of the day before fading away with his elaborate flourishes. Music had always been something that lifted my soul, and today was no exception. I let myself slip into the chords and be carried away by the joy of praise for just a few minutes.

After the service and a wonderful sermon about the way God's love reaches down to us even when we don't reach back, I felt much more grounded and even safer than I had the day before. Plus, somewhere in my mind I could feel something getting worked out about Ms. Orlan's death, and while I knew better than to try and rush that process, I was glad to feel some answers coming along.

I had let Mary know the situation the night before because I wasn't sure who would be at her house for her usual Sunday lunch and wanted to know what she thought about talking about the old school with those folks. True to form, Mary had quickly responded and said everyone who was already invited would love to talk about the school and that she'd see if she could get a couple of the church elders to join us, too.

And sure enough, when we began the walk up the street to her house for chicken and dumplings and collards, a meal I loved with something fundamental in my soul, she told me that two of the older women in the church had accepted her invitation and knew that I was going to be there to listen to their stories about the school. "You brought your notebook, right?"

I smiled and tugged the small moleskin out of one back pocket and a digital recorder out of the other. "Always." I leaned over and gave her a side hug. "Thank you."

"Of course, but before we go in," she stopped me on the sidewalk just before her house and said, "Are you okay? This is a lot to delve into, and you're walking some fine lines, as I know you know, in this situation. You getting enough rest?"

I smiled. "I am, but I appreciate your concern. And today, if I start to cross any lines I shouldn't, you'll give me a signal?"

"If I bring in the coconut cake, it means stop talking," she said with a grin.

"So are you saying I need to venture across lines to get dessert? Because I can do that." I laughed.

"No, ma'am. I'll invite you for cake once you have some good info, but I'll interrupt with it if need be." She took my hand and walked with me up onto her porch. "Sound good?"

"Perfect," I said. "As long as I get my cake."

For the next few minutes, she and I did the last bit of prep for lunch, including dishing out the two crock-pots of goodness into serving bowls and making sure there was plenty of ice in every glass. No one wanted warm water or warm iced tea on a day this hot.

———

8

The food at Mary's was as good as it always was, and by the time I was done with the dumplings and a second helping of collards, I was even more motivated to not cross any lines into ill-taste or disrespect because I needed time before I ate that coconut cake. Not eating it was simply out of the question.

So when we sat down to talk in Mary's living room after eating, I made a point to be as truthful as I could, within the boundaries to protect the investigation that Santiago had set out this morning, and explained that we were looking for more information about the woman whose body had been found under the school house.

The two elders who had joined us didn't waste any time telling their stories. Mrs. Marines went first and explained how she had been a student there. "Enid here was smart for her age, so even though she's just a baby, we were in the same class."

I looked over at Enid Brown and smiled. "A baby, huh?"

"She's called me that since we were girls. "I'm only a year younger," she said with a wink.

I laughed. "Spring chickens, both of you," I said before

asking if they had any stories they'd like to share about Ms. Agee. I had to make a decided effort to call her by her assumed name since I had now fully begun to think of her as Ethel Orlan.

And so began a delightful two hours of women riffing off one another, teasing one another, and reminiscing about their school, their friends, and their teacher, a woman they both adored and felt so sad to have not had more time with.

"She was just stellar and kind. I see those teachers on those videos hugging their students or dancing with them when they come in," Enid said. "They always remind me of Ms. Agee. That kind of thing wasn't acceptable in those days, mind you, but she always greeted us by name and made a point to spend some one-on-one time with each of us every day."

"Wow," I said. "That is impressive."

"It is," Mrs. Marines added, "but we didn't know that then. She made it seem normal, to be expected that we were considered important." She patted the tight curls on her head and said, "It wasn't until I had other teachers who weren't quite as skilled that I realized Ms. Agee had been something special."

On that note, Enid stood carefully to her feet and extended her hand to her friend. "Are you ready, dear?" she asked.

Mrs. Marines stood and took her hand. "Always, with you." Then she leaned over and kissed Enid.

The surprise must have been written on my face because Mrs. Marines looked at me and said, "Don't be surprised, Ms. Sutton. We've been around far longer than you have."

Then, they walked out the door hand-in-hand, and I smiled as I watched them walk up the street. "Wow, that's the second gay couple who had Ms. Agee as a teacher. How fortunate they were to have her."

"Absolutely," Mary said as the rest of us headed into the kitchen for the coconut cake that Mrs. Marines and Enid had refused because they were on their way to dinner with other friends. "They're quite the couple, super social, too."

"I gather. I'm worn out just from hanging out with you." Everyone laughed, and headed back to the table, where the cake was waiting.

I savored a huge slice of cake and then lingered around while everyone else gathered their things and headed out after thanking Mary for a delicious meal. I typically stayed behind to help wash dishes and return Mary's table to its smaller size, but today I also wanted to talk to her about what we'd learned that day.

As I returned the butter to the fridge and grabbed the dishrag to wash down the table, I asked, "Do you think it's odd that there were two same-sex couples in Ms. Agee's school?"

Mary smiled. "I expect some people might, but I'm of the mind that there were probably a whole lot more gay folks about than we knew back then but it wasn't safe for them to show their true feelings. I expect Ms. Agee – I mean Ms. Orlan – just made them feel safe."

What she said rang true. "I heard Glennon Doyle say something similar once, and that makes sense to me." I moved from the table to the counters after rinsing the rag. "But if the students knew she was what we'd now call 'affirming,' surely some folks in town didn't like that."

"Oh, I'm sure they didn't. Fair number of folks don't appreciate Enid and Bea's relationship now. You should have seen the ruckus when they were elected to the Deacon Board." She shook her head. "You'd have thought we suggested the devil himself lead the church."

I sighed. I hoped that when Sawyer was older that this kind of prejudice and hatred would be a thing of history, but some days I didn't have much hope for that. "It was great to hear their stories, but I don't know that it got us any further into figuring out who killed Ms. Orlan."

Mary took the rag from me, rinsed it, and then pointed toward the living room. "I might have someone who can help. He'll be here in just a minute."

I looked at my friend but took the fresh glass of iced tea she offered and followed her back to the living room. We sat quietly, sipping our tea and enjoying the silence that two friends can share, when her doorbell sounded. Before Mary could stand, someone walked in and said, "Hello."

I stood up to greet the guest and felt my face break open into a wide smile when I saw Foster Grant standing there. "Mr. Grant, it's good to see you again."

Mary hugged the older man and then said, "We have a situation we could use your help with, Foster."

He looked from her and to me and then back again. "Does this have to do with Ms. Agee?"

I nodded. "Yes, sir. I've just met Enid and Bea."

"Ah, so yes, you now know that there were two gay couples in her school, and if you thought it might have caused problems for her to be so accepting of Rufus and I, then you think someone might have been extra angry since Bea and Enid were involved, too." He completed my thought perfectly.

"I thought since you are the person with the most knowledge of the LGBTQ community here in Octonia you might have some sense of whether or not someone back then might have been angry enough to hurt, um, Ms. Agee." Mary's face flushed as she caught herself before using the teacher's real name.

Foster looked at her and nodded. "Unfortunately, there's probably not a shortage of suspects from back then, but most of the people who could have done this are dead." He turned his gaze to me. "Is it worth it to stir this up? If you tell me it is, I will gladly help, but I want you both to be sure of what you might be doing here."

"Are you saying folks might be upset now if we delve into

this?" I asked, remembering Mary's words about when Enid and Bea had become deacons.

"Yes, ma'am, I am. And not just the people you might expect. There's a reason Mary invited me here alone today." He held my gaze while I caught on.

"Rufus? He doesn't want this angle of her death explored?" I asked.

"He would rather we leave all of those hard years behind, you see. It wasn't pretty, and we are simply of two different minds about how to handle that history. I believe we need to talk about it. He believes we need to move past it." Foster let out a long slow breath.

"If I may, though, how do we move past it if we don't talk about it?" I said and quickly hoped I hadn't stepped too far.

"That is exactly my point, Ms. Sutton. So if you are ready, let's talk." He studied my face a minute, and when I nodded, he began. "The first person we need to talk about is Shelley O'Hara."

I stared at him and then swallowed. "Okay," I said and then waited.

"Shelley is not homophobic in the least, and her father was not either. But her mother, well, her mother was another story," Foster began. He then went on to regale us with tales about how Mrs. Stone had followed him and Rufus home from school shouting things about how they were going to burn in hell and suffer eternal torment. "She was relentless. It got so bad that we had to have our parents come and walk us home." He shook his head.

As I thought about these two little boys walking down the road with someone screaming such hate at them, tears sprang to my eyes. "Oh, Mr. Grant, I'm so sorry." I let the sadness of that experience sit in the room for a minute, and then I asked, "Does Shelley know her mother did that?"

Foster nodded. "She was there, holding her mother's hand."

He cleared his throat. "In some ways, I think what her mother did hurt her worse than it did us."

"But Shelley didn't accept what her mother said?" I asked as I thought about how readily Sawyer picked up on the things his father and I said about other people, be those things good or bad.

"Her father saw to that. Made sure Rufus, Shelley, and I all played together and talked. Took us out to dinner. Reminded us all that we were just kids who deserved to be treated kindly." Foster smiled. "Between him and Ms. Agee, we turned out okay. Not sure what any of us would be like if they hadn't been there."

I smiled at him softly. "Thank goodness for good people," I whispered.

"Thank God," Mary said, and Foster nodded.

"So we need to talk to Shelley about this?" I asked.

When Foster nodded, I felt my heart thump. That wasn't going to be a fun conversation. "Okay, I'll tell Santiago. Anyone else you think we should investigate?"

He nodded. "I expect you've talked to Marvin Simon?"

"The former student everyone thought she was having an affair with?" I asked.

"That's the one. There's a lot more to their relationship than most folks know. Marvin is gay, and Ms. Agee knew that. She was trying to help him, guide him a little to keep him safe but also to let him know that what he felt was completely normal and good." Foster shook his head. "But Marvin couldn't accept it. His parents had kicked him out when he'd said he was interested in boys, and their hatred had already broken his heart."

"Poor man," I said but then looked at Foster and frowned. "Wouldn't that make him less likely to kill Ms. Agee, though?"

"Not necessarily," Mary said. "Marvin has become a very active supporter of conversion therapy."

"That nonsense about making people un-gay?" I asked.

"Exactly," Foster said. "His hatred toward himself has turned outward. I don't know exactly where he was with things back then, but it might be worth asking some questions."

I nodded and pushed the thoughts swarming around in my head to the back so I could concentrate on what else Foster might have to tell me. "Finally, you will want to talk to Terrance Harlow again. He told me the sheriff already spoke to him, but he didn't tell you everything. I don't know exactly what he withheld, but he did say that if the sheriff came to speak with him again, he would feel obliged to share what he knew."

I sighed. "Santiago felt pretty sure that Harlow didn't kill Ms. Agee, so this will be discouraging."

"Oh, don't get me wrong," Foster said as he stood and put on his ball cap. "I don't think Harlow killed her. But he may know who did."

"Thank you, Mr. Grant," I said. "So much."

"If any of it helps find out who killed that wonderful woman, I will be glad to have shared. But please, if you would, keep me out of the discussions. I don't mind, but I don't want to cause Rufus any more pain if I can help it."

"Understood," I said and reached up to give him a hug. "Thank you again."

He smiled and showed himself out. I dropped into the couch beside Mary and said, "Oh, this just gets uglier and uglier. I kind of understand why Rufus just wants to let bygones be bygones."

"Me, too, but of course, they aren't really bygone, are they?" Mary said as she leaned against me. "And somebody is still invested in keeping Ms. Agee's death a secret, otherwise you wouldn't be so worried."

I slumped against my friend. "You ever watch TV?"

"Woman, today, we are watching something ridiculous. How do you feel about the new season of *Riverdale*?" she asked.

"Perfect," I said. Nothing felt more fitting than a quite-dark, modern remake on a mid-century comic book. Just absurd and weird enough to fit the odd twists and turns that this query had taken in the past few days.

We had just finished the first episode when Mary's doorbell rang. This time, the visitor waited until she came to the door before he came in, and I was very glad to see it was Santiago. I was getting pretty sleepy, and I was really eager to see what Shelley had told him, and I couldn't wait to tell him about what Foster had told us about Shelley's mom.

Mary got him a glass of iced tea and then took her seat on the couch. "Well?" she said. "Is there anything you can share?"

He nodded. "Everything, actually. She was completely surprised to read the letters from her father, but she did confirm that they were written in his handwriting." He shook his head. "Her surprise made me rethink the letters again."

I sat for a second and watched his face as he tried to piece things together, and my resolve to wait until he had shared all he had learned before telling him what Foster had said deteriorated. "I think we may be able to help with that."

I quickly filled him in about Mrs. Stone and about how Mr. Stone had defended Rufus and Grant and, likely, Enid and Bea. "A kind man like that, it doesn't seem likely that he'd threaten a teacher does it?" I was asking sincerely because while I had a theory about the letters, it wasn't my job to develop the theories. That work was for Santiago and Savannah.

He nodded. "That lines up with what I'm learning and what my instincts are saying. Plus, there's something Savannah found out today that might help, too. While I was talking to Shelley, she looked through her father's date book to see if anything had been written down for the weekend that Ms. Agee went missing. And lo and behold, he had been out of town, in Lancaster, Pennsylvania, of all places, that very weekend."

"Lancaster? Why?" Mary asked.

"Not sure. The note just said, Lancaster, PA – EO." It was like saying the letters fired a synapse in his brain because Santi's eyes lit up. "EO – Ethel Orlan. It has to be."

I stared at him and nodded. I knew he was right, but I wasn't making all the connections yet. He was in Lancaster to do something for Ms. Orlan?"

Santiago stood up and put his hand palm out in front of us. "Go with me on this, okay?"

Mary and I nodded and sat forward.

"What if Mr. Stone had gone to Lancaster to find Ms. Orlan a place to live? Maybe a new job? What if he was out of town to get her set up?" Santiago's voice grew excited.

Mary leaned back and looked up at the ceiling. "That could be, but then wouldn't he have found it odd to come back and find her gone?"

"You're assuming that the plan was for him to come back, give her the details, and then for her to go, right?" I asked as Mary nodded. "But what if the plan had been for her to follow him there that same weekend, the weekend she had told everyone she was going out of town."

Santiago was shifting his weight from foot to foot. "And so he didn't think much of it when he came back and she was already gone. And since she and he had built a cover story about him wanting her out of town, a story that could be backed up by the letters he sent, he thought she was in the clear."

I sighed. "He'd have had no way of checking on her to be sure everything was okay without risking exposure, so he must have never known she died."

"But that still leaves one big question, though," Mary said.

"Why did someone kill her?" I said.

"And why was she hiding in the first place?" Santiago added.

I sighed. "We're not closer to knowing who killed Ms.

Orlan, but at least we know, fairly certainly, that it wasn't Humphrey Stone." I tried to take some relief from the fact that the kind man everyone loved was actually who he portrayed himself to be, but I couldn't get past the sadness I felt about the fact that this woman had died and no one, not even the man working to protect her, had known it. Not for decades.

THE RIDE HOME to my house that night was quiet as each of us tried to process what we'd learned and let ourselves feel the way we did about the ever-deepening sorrow around Ethel Orlan's death. I was deep in thought when we pulled into my driveway, so it took me a minute to register what I was seeing. But as soon as I did, I was out of the car and screaming.

Someone had spray painted a homophobic slur on the side of my beautiful house in the most nasty red color. The entire end of my farmhouse was covered in red letters that were almost as tall as I was, and while I screamed and swore and kicked at sticks in the yard, the tears started to pour down my face. "Who would do this to my house? Who would attack something so beautiful with such hate?"

Santiago let me rage and shout for a long while, and when I started to calm, he said, "We'll take care of this tonight. Let me make a couple of calls."

I heard what he said, and I knew he was going to fix things. But I couldn't really process anything. I was just so angry – angry and hurt – and scared. Very scared. This wasn't the first time my house had been threatened, but each time something happened here, at my sanctuary, I felt it more deeply.

Dad had suggested a while ago that I think about actually using the gate that had been put up by the previous owners when the house had been unoccupied. At the time I had shrugged him off, but now I was wondering. At the very least, I was going to put up a game camera and a driveway alarm so that I knew who was coming in and out – and when.

I finally calmed a bit and sat down on the stairs to the house while Santiago opened the door, went in, and let Beauregard slip out. Poor cat must have heard the intruders out here and not been able to do anything. Now, he was just rubbing against my arm over and over again, and I didn't know if it was to comfort me or himself. Probably both. I pulled him into my lap and buried my face in his fur.

"Your Dad and Lucille are on their way as are Dom, Mika, and Savannah. You had this paint in your garage," he held up a can, "and I think it matches. We'll have to repaint the whole side, but it shouldn't be noticeably different from the rest of the house."

I sighed. "Thank you, but you guys don't have to do this. I can scrub it off." I meant what I said, but just looking at the giant, hate-filled writing made me want to cry again.

"No, no you can't, Paisley. Let us help you." He pulled me close and let me sob into his shirt for a few more minutes. Then he said, "I poured you a glass of wine. Go get it while I take some pictures and samples. We need the evidence before we can clean it up."

I nodded. *Evidence.* Someone had committed a crime here. Just realizing that made me feel better somehow. This was very much a personal attack, an attack on a place I felt safe, but I wasn't the only one who thought so. This was a crime. A recognizable crime.

The wine Santiago had poured me was just what I needed, cold and crisp and fermented. And I sat on the porch and watched him make notes, take measurements, snap photos, and then scrape paint samples. By the time he was done, Savannah had arrived with Mika and Dom right behind. They didn't waste any time grabbing the rollers and paint brushes Santiago had gotten out of the garage, and Dom set up the 25-foot ladder that had come with the house and climbed to the top.

Dad and Lucille showed up shortly after with four pizzas, more wine, and a chocolate cake that looked to contain enough cocoa to power a small city. It was perfect. As Lucille and I set up the food, the other four kept painting and quickly too. When I went out to suggest a break and some food, they had already covered up the letters F and A and well on to obscuring the G from view as well. Now, my house looked like it said, "Lover" on it, and that wasn't nearly as awful.

While I managed to eat a piece of pizza, I thought about leaving the word "lover" on the house as a signal that I wasn't intimidated and a reminder that I wasn't ashamed to love anyone. Ever. But I couldn't figure out how I'd explain the presence of graffiti on our house to Sawyer, and when I thought about how hard I'd have to work to keep him from adding to it, I knew we'd be painting everything over.

The idea of a four-year-old with a spray paint can tagging his own home made me laugh though, and when I shared the vision with my friends and family, we all got to giggling so hard that Mika actually sprayed wine out her nose. That, in turn, broke us up again, and soon the seven of us were laughing so hard that Beauregard actually meowed in protest.

After that, the work went quickly, eased along by a fair portion of wine for each of us, and by the time we were done painting, we were actually enjoying ourselves so much that we decided to light a fire in the firepit and relax together in the mildly cooler evening.

Dom and Mika had been all business while we painted, but now they were the cuddle king and queen, all arms and legs wrapped up in each other. It was very cute, and I was glad to see their date on the parkway had gone well.

We talked for a while about our days, about the ingredients in Lucille's chocolate cake, which included so much butter that we'd probably all need bypass surgery soon, and about the gift that a summer evening with friends was. What we didn't talk about was the situation around Ms. Orlan's death. It was just too much tonight, and while I knew we were all wondering who cared enough about what I was researching to defile my house with such ugliness, I appreciated that we all decided to forego further conversation in that direction for the evening. I just needed this time at this place to make me feel safe and secure here again, and friends and fire were just the thing to do it.

9

That night, I was grateful that Santiago stayed over, mostly because I wasn't sure I would have slept if he hadn't. We went to bed early, my nerves too frazzled for me to even work on my cross-stitch, even though I knew doing so would settle me.

And when I woke up the next morning, I didn't feel much better. But Sawyer was coming home today, and I needed to pull myself together. I took a long shower while Santiago made us baked oatmeal, and then I put on make-up, dressed in something I enjoyed wearing, and spent the next couple of hours tidying the house while Santiago worked in the living room.

Our plan was to wait for Sawyer to get home and then all head into town where Saw and I would work at my shop, with Saul nearby, until dinner time. Then, we would go to Santi's for dinner, a treat for Saw for sure, before coming back home for bedtime, all three of us.

Sawyer was definitely going to have a lot of questions about Santi sleeping over. But since I had already given his father a heads up about Santi providing police protection, without the details of the case behind it, I knew that at least his father wouldn't think I was violating our agreement to talk with one another if a significant other was staying over when Saw was there. In fact, his dad had been grateful to Santi for keeping an eye on all of us.

Truthfully, I had thought about suggesting Sawyer stay with his dad, an offer his father had also graciously extended, but I knew his dad had to work. Plus, it was important to Saw that he have a routine and get to see both of us regularly. Santiago would be nearby, and Dad and Lucille had made a point of clearing their schedules for the next few days, too, just in case. We would be fine.

Of course, as soon as Saw came home, he jumped into Santiago's arms. His dad wasn't thrilled with that choice, I could tell, but to his credit, he smiled and shook Santi's hand before saying goodbye and walking toward his car. I walked with him while Sawyer showed Santiago his room, as if the man had not just slept there, and explained to my ex that I'd check in regularly for the next couple of days so he didn't worry.

He thanked me and then headed off to work while I walked back inside to snuggle my little boy before bustling him off to town. Santiago had suggested we could stay here today, but I still had a business to run. And no one was going to intimidate me out of taking care of myself and my son. So while I was a bit nervous about leaving the house unattended, I took heart that the game camera Dad had put up before we even got out of bed this morning would let us know if someone came.

Plus, I wasn't about to leave Beauregard home alone again. I'd leashed him and loaded him as soon as Sawyer was in the car. The cat settled into Sawyer's lap as soon as the door shut. Such a hardship for both of them.

And when I suggested to Sawyer that he swing the gate shut for the day, something he'd been asking to do for weeks, he climbed up it and held on as he kicked off the fence and rode the gate to the other post. Santi locked the chain around the post and gate and then handed me the key. It wasn't Fort Knox, but it would be much harder for anyone to come, at least in a vehicle, toward my house, and today, that was going to have to be enough.

The drive into town was chatty as Sawyer told us all about hurricanes and fire tornados, phenomenon that I only knew existed because my son had, somehow, become obsessed with them. We learned about how we could hide in things that were brick but not wood, and that if a hurricane was coming, we stay away from water, but "if there's a fire tornado, you need to run to the water," Sawyer said as he waved his pointed finger at me in the rearview mirror. "That is very important," he said.

"Got it, Saw," I said. "Run away from water for hurricanes. Run toward it for fire tornados."

"What about volcanoes?" Santiago asked, and I shot him a look that said, *Don't encourage him.*

But Sawyer was ready with an answer. "Run. As fast as you can. Nothing will save you if the lava gets you." His voice was so serious, and I made a decision that we might curb our viewing of videos about natural disasters for a while.

We dropped Santiago off at the station, and then Saw, Beau, and I drove straight to the shop, where I immediately texted Santi to let him know we were safe and checked in with Saul. Mika's uncle wasn't alone though. He'd held a couple of his crew back on the lot just in case, he said. And I thanked them all.

"Besides," one of the guys said, "who else is going to give Sawyer excavator lessons if we're not here?"

"What?!" Sawyer said as he jumped up and down. "Mom, I'm going to drive an excavator today. I'll check in on you later." And then he and the guys were off to a dirt pile at the back of the lot.

"Thank you, Saul," I said. "From both of us."

He nodded. "You okay, Paisley girl?"

I sighed. "Mostly, I think. Glad to have some work to do, though. Keep my mind off things."

"Well, I'm right here, and the guys are watching the gate. You need us you just call, okay?" Saul stood up and patted me on the back as I walked out the door. He was such a good guy.

As I went back to the shop, I saw that Beauregard had taken up his usual perch on the dashboard of the car. I had left the windows open and put a little kibble and a bowl of water in the back for him. But I knew he would mostly nap in the sun and watch the birds all day. What a terrible life he had.

Around the side of the shop, I took a look around at my large-scale inventory. The lot of wood that Claire had sold on Saturday was flagged and ready to load whenever the buyer sent a truck. I'd look for that information when I got inside.

The other two wood lots I had available were carefully stacked under the lean-to beside my shop with the plow that Claire had also sold and a few other larger pieces, including two church pews that I had salvaged from my own church when we had needed to make more wheelchair-accessible seating. I didn't have a lot of space out here in the roof-covered lot, so I made a note to talk with Saul about other options for storage, like another lean-to on the other side of the shed that housed my shop.

Inside, I noted that the buyers were coming for the wood today and that it looked like pick-up was also scheduled for the plow. That was good news for my revenue stream and also for my space requirements. I had a salvage job at an old hunting shack up in the mountains scheduled for this Friday and Saturday, and I was going to need space for that new selection of wood, some of which I was told was wormy chestnut. If that information was accurate, that wood was going to sell for a pretty penny given how rare it was.

All of this was great news since I was hoping to hire another shopkeeper to work sales for Mika and me at the city market in Charlottesville this fall. We'd done really well there last year, and I was glad it looked like we'd be able to keep business going and even growing a little on three fronts, the shop, the market, and my salvage jobs.

Soon, I'd be able to do pay rent to Saul like I wanted to for the use of his lot. He kept insisting that the space sat empty if I wasn't using it and that my presence made his work space more homey and welcoming to guests, and I know those things were true. But I also knew that I wanted to honor his space and pay him something, even if it would still be far less than it would cost me to open a storefront elsewhere.

Between running my numbers, tending to the customers who stopped by for incidental items and to pick up their bigger purchases, and keeping an eye on Sawyer from time to time, I was quite busy for the first couple of hours of the day. But once I'd cut a check for Mika's items that had sold, run to the bank with my deposit, and balanced my books, I was fresh out of stuff to do and the worries of the past few days rushed back in.

But I had learned that rather than perseverate on problems, I needed to work through them. Today, that meant taking out my notebook, jotting down the words "Perseveration List" and then taking a brief minute to enjoy the beauty of the word *perseverate* before I began to write.

I made a note of all we knew about Ethel Orlan, including her approximate death date, an estimated age, and her character traits, including a genuine support for her LGBTQ students. Then, I wrote down suspects, including Humphrey Stone, even though I immediately crossed through his name. The list was short but meaningful – Marvin Simon, Mrs. Stone, Terrance Harlow, and potentially someone from her past who scared her. I had my doubts about Terrance, given what Foster Grant and Santi had said, but I didn't want to eliminate him from contention completely.

Then, I went full-on into brainstorming on the questions I still had:

1. How did Hortense Agee and Ethel Orlan meet?
2. Why was Ethel Orlan hiding and from whom?
3. Who had killed Ethel? Was that person the same as the person she was hiding from? Or was it someone different?

I figured Ms. Nicholas might have figured out the answer to my first question during her time with Ms. Key and Angelia the day before, so I took out my phone and gave her a ring.

She answered on the first ring and sounded truly happy to hear from me. "I do have some information that might be useful," she said as I picked up my pen again.

"Hit me," I said.

"Okay, so Hortense did go to Hampton, as Alva told us. She worked as a resident assistant her last two years, and when I did a little digging, I was able to find a freshman named Ethel Orlan in Hortense's dorm." Ms. Nicholas paused.

"Well, that answers one of my questions. They knew each other from college. Great. That's good information." I made a note about this fact next to the question.

"But also, when I called Hampton this morning to inquire about Ms. Orlan's records, the woman at the registrar's office said she could only release those to a family member. When I explained that Ms. Orlan had no living family members that we knew of but that we had recently discovered her remains here in Octonia, she opened right up."

"Ooh," I said and poised my pen over my paper. "Do tell."

"Well, apparently, Ms. Orlan had a sort of stalker situation, although that wasn't the term they used then, it seems. The registrar said her file read that she had an "unwelcome caller." Apparently, Ethel had called campus police on several occasions because she'd seen a man following her or waiting in the shadows outside her door."

My heart was racing. "That is terrifying. Did they catch him?"

"No." Ms. Nicholas said, and I could hear the disgust in her voice. "According to her file, she couldn't identify the man because she'd never seen his face, and so they thought she was just, and I quote, 'being hysterical.'"

My fear turned quickly to rage. "Oh, if I knew the name of those officers, I'd be down to Tidewater this afternoon—"

Ms. Nicholas cut me off. "We actually do know their names, but I already pursued the 'hunt them down and scare the life out of them' angle, and they are both deceased. Apparently, God got to them before we could."

I chuckled. "Well, I trust that God has things well in hand then."

"Indeed she does," Ms. Nicholas said. "But there's more to the story. Shortly after the last complaint was filed, about three weeks before the end of Ethel's final term, she withdrew from Hampton and left without a word."

I huffed. "She went into hiding."

"That's my perception, too." Ms. Nicholas sighed heavily. "We can't know for sure, of course, but I expect this is when she reached out to Ms. Agee."

I nodded and then realized Ms. Nicholas couldn't see me. "Yes, I agree. I think that's a safe assumption to make." I took a deep breath. "So now we know why she went into hiding, and we can assume that when she told Ms. Agee she'd been found out, that the person who was stalking her had found her."

"Yes, yes, I think, so, too," Ms. Nicholas said. "So only two questions remain, as I see it."

"Who was stalking her, and did he kill her?"

"Precisely," she said. The line grew silent for a few moments, and then she said, "You'll tell Santiago."

"I will," I said.

"Thank you, dear." Then she clicked off without another word.

I looked down at my phone for a minute and then immediately called Santiago. He answered on the first ring. "Paisley?"

"I'm fine, but I just spoke with Ms. Nicholas. She found out some good information." I gave him the update about Ms. Orlan's time at Hampton and about her stalker. "So we know more now," I said in conclusion.

Santi didn't respond.

"You okay?" I said.

He sighed. "Oh yeah, sorry. I was just thinking about what Mika said the other day, about how our systems don't protect women until it's too late. Case in point."

"It's true, but we also live under a system that says innocent until proven guilty. I'm not sure we want to give that up."

"True, but maybe we could begin by just believing women when they tell us something is wrong." He sounded frustrated and a bit angry.

"I'm not going to disagree with you there, but you do believe women. I know. I've seen you believe us. I've seen you take action as best you can within the confines of the law." I didn't really know a way to make him feel better because he was right. The system and the way people thought of violence against women was messed up. But he wasn't responsible. In fact, he was part of the solution. "Let's solve this case, okay? And get Ethel Orlan some justice."

I heard him let out a long stream of breath. "Okay. I still need to follow up with Marvin Simon and Terrance Harlow given what Foster told you yesterday, so I'm headed over to see Simon now. You okay there for a couple more hours?"

I strolled outside and watched Sawyer maneuver the bucket of an excavator into the deep hole he and his team had already dug. "Oh yeah, we're just fine. Don't wear your good shoes when you come to get us though, okay? Sawyer has something to show you."

"Alright," he said with enthusiasm. "Talk to you soon."

I hung up and went over to watch my boy do his work. People often marveled at his dexterity and thought I was exaggerating when I described what he could do with his body, but this boy understood the mechanics of his own anatomy and of machines so well. One of Saul's crew members was in the cab with him, and I assumed that man was working the foot pedals. But Saw was controlling the bucket's motion by himself, and he was good. He was using the scoop to widen the hole little by little, and when he had enough dirt accumulated at the bottom of the pit, he scooped it up and put it to the side.

I felt Saul walk up next to me. "At this rate," he said, "He'll be at the earth's core by closing time."

"Don't give him any ideas," I said. "Thanks for this."

"Are you kidding? My guys are loving it. Neither of them has kids, but I know they both want them. This is scratching that itch a little."

"They in a position to have kids?" I asked, careful not to make assumptions about marriage or orientation with my question.

"Both of them are stable. One is married to a woman, but they're having trouble. In treatments and all that. The other is gay, and his husband and he are in the process of adopting. It's going to be a long road for both of them, but they'll both make great dads."

I looked over at the two burly, bearded men who were laughing just as hard as my son was as he moved dirt out of the hole. There was no doubt of that fact.

BY THE END of the day, I was in a far better mood than I had been earlier. Part of that was due to seeing Sawyer really enjoy his time in the excavator and then watching him build his own, much smaller, hole on the side of the shop when he grew tired of the big machine. He played by himself for almost an hour, and it was lovely to hear him singing and talking to himself.

But I was also buoyed because the customer stream had been busy that afternoon. We'd sold a number of doorknobs to a woman who was fixing up one of the old Victorians in town and wanted to match the remaining crystal originals, and I'd also managed to convince an older gentleman that he could, in fact, make a belt from a lot of square topped nails I'd salvaged from an old community hardware store about a year ago. He promised to send me pictures when he was done, and I looked forward to seeing the eighty-ton belt when it was finished.

Between those sales and the customers who came in and bought various corbels and hand-knit items from Mika, we were busy all afternoon. I wasn't going to make my living off these kind of stop-in sales, but they did help build some cushion into the business for the days when the big lots weren't moving.

When Santiago pulled up in my car just before five, I smiled and shouted for Sawyer to come. Saul and his guys had stayed around, filling the hole Sawyer had dug, so that Saw could show Santi his new excavator skills. And true to form, Santi had worn his work boots and old jeans with his uniform shirt on top.

"Your mom said you were doing something amazing today, Saw-guy," Santi said as he caught my son in mid-leap. "Will you show me?"

"Of course," Sawyer said and pointed toward the back of the lot. The three of us walked that way, and just as we did, one of guys started up the excavator.

Sawyer jumped down from Santi's arms and shouted, "Wait for me, Dave" as he sprinted for the cab and climbed into it like he'd been doing it all his life.

As we watched, Saw proceeded to re-empty part of the hole the guys had just filled, and Santi was genuinely impressed with his skills. "You might have a neurosurgeon on your hands, Pais," he said.

"I don't think they have big equipment in operating rooms," I said.

"True," he answered, "but they do have robots." He raised his eyebrows and then winked at me.

"You may have a point." I smiled as Saw dug two more scoops of dirt before the guys called it quits for the night. "But if he wants to run an excavator, then I'll support him. Fewer loans involved."

"You're a good mom," Santiago said as he gave me a quick hug. "You'll stand behind him no matter what. I know that."

It was amazing how wonderful the sentence, "You are a good mom" felt to me. I didn't doubt myself all that much, but sometimes, all the 'shoulds' and 'oughts' of parenting got to me. To be reminded that I was doing a good job was a huge boost most days.

Sawyer was quite excited by the idea of steaks at Santi's house for dinner, but given his busy day, we had to play a rousing game of 'I Spy' to keep him awake. Beauregard was not amused by our shouting or over the top spying since, apparently, seven solid hours of sleep in the sun was not quite enough for him, but he managed to tolerate the situation until we got to Santi's house.

But on arrival there, as I unloaded him and Santi unstrapped Saw, the cat coughed up the nastiest hairball I had ever seen as if to say, "Torture me that way again, and I can make these things all day." I swear he was a mafia boss in a former life.

Once we'd all gotten inside, I got Sawyer a cup of juice and sent him and Beau into the backyard with a soccer ball. I felt a little mean telling Saw to try to hit Beau with the ball, but I knew the cat was far too fast to allow such a thing to happen. And besides, he had to understand the consequences of coughing up nastiness like that right on my shoe.

Inside, Santi seasoned the steaks he had set out to thaw when he came by mid-day, and I popped three baked potatoes into the microwave bag that made them taste like oven-baked. Saw wasn't going to make it another hour for us to cook them in the oven, and honestly, I was starving and didn't want to wait that long either.

Once the potatoes were in and the steaks on, I mixed up a green salad from the various things I had sent home with Santiago from our garden and set the table while my boyfriend went outside to save Beau a direct hit now that he was fatiguing a bit.

I poured us both a glass of wine but then stayed inside with mine as I watched my boys from the window. They laughed and leaped, and while I knew they were both exhausted, I could also tell neither of them would pass up these few minutes of fun for any amount of rest in the world.

I, however, was glad of the downtime and enjoyed watching them while I sipped. Beauregard watched from the safety of a patio chair and cleaned himself again, no doubt preparing another hairball to teach me a lesson.

10

W e listened to some Ed Sheeran on the way home, one of Sawyer's favorites and a happy concession to the pop music both Santiago and I usually avoided. We weren't ten minutes into the drive when Sawyer fell asleep, and given that he was now such a sound sleeper, I didn't even try to wake him. We'd just carry him in when we got home.

But when we pulled up to my driveway, home suddenly seemed so far away. Someone, apparently with a very heavy-duty vehicle, had rammed the gate to my house hard enough to bend it and pull the post to which it was chained halfway out of the ground. The sheer force of the hits revealed just how angry or determined this person was, and it was terrifying.

I was very glad Sawyer was asleep as Santi put the car in park and got out with his phone already to his ear, no doubt calling Savannah to update her.

A large part of me wanted to simply stay in the car and maybe even go to sleep like my son, but the other part of me was furious and needed to take a closer look. So once Santiago had gone up the driveway and checked to be sure the house was secure, I stepped out of the car and looked around.

The damage was extensive, and the gate would have to be taken to recycling or sold for scrap metal. It was unusable, which was saying something given how heavy duty cattle gates like this one were. The red paint of the gate had been gouged out in several places, and when I looked closely, I could see flakes of silver shining on the bars.

I pointed to those, and Santiago nodded. "Not sure if they're the raw metal from under the gate's paint or flakes from the vehicle that hit it, but we'll take samples for sure."

The base of the post that had come out of the ground held up six inches of concrete. It had been quite snugly in the earth until someone had tried to ram it loose. The other post was still secure, but I imagined I'd need to replace both just to be certain everything was solid. And I would be doing that, certainly. This gate was going to be permanently closed from now on, and I was going to fence off the areas around it, too, so someone couldn't just walk down the drive.

I sighed. I didn't have the funds or the energy to do this kind of home security, but apparently, it was going to be necessary. I knew Dad and Lucille would help me with the money if I needed help, and Santi would certainly work with me on securing things. But I was so weary of having to ask the people I loved for help.

"Pais," Santi called softly. "Come look at this."

I walked over to where he stood behind my car. "Tire marks?"

"Those weren't there this morning, right?"

"Nope. Sometimes the garbage truck makes marks when it turns around here, but nothing like this." I looked closely. "Did someone peel out here?"

"Looks like it." He looked up and down the road. "I wonder

if someone drove up while this was happening. That would explain why they didn't finish the job."

"And why they left in a hurry." I took out my phone and logged into the neighborhood app I had installed. "Okay if I ask if anyone saw anything?"

"Definitely. Ask them to let you know and if they are okay giving me a statement," he said as he used his phone to measure the tire marks.

I typed up my message and took a photo of the damage. Almost as soon as my message went up, a reply came through. "Was hoping you'd post here. I was going to come down later to check on you," the neighbor from across the tracks wrote. "Be there in five."

"The neighbor is on his way." I pointed across the way to his farmstead, where two huge bulls were napping in the grass.

"Good. Let's get this gate open and put that little boy to bed." Santiago took the key I handed him and unlocked the chain. It felt a little silly since we could have probably pushed over the post and dragged it to the side, but I appreciated the imagined security he was allowing me to have.

When Santi lifted Sawyer out of his seat, the little boy instinctively wrapped his legs around the man and put his head on his shoulder. If the night hadn't been so jarring, I would have taken a picture of them. Instead, I just kissed Saw lightly on the cheek and suggested Santi simply take off his pants and shoes and let him sleep in his shirt.

Then, while they were upstairs, I got the whiskey back out, found the orange juice, and poured three glasses. This night required a certain kind of sustenance.

As I finished, I saw my neighbor, Tom, walking up the road and went out onto the porch to meet him. "Sawyer just went to bed. Mind if we talk on the front porch?"

"Not at all. Glad you got the gate open. Wasn't sure you'd be able to," he said as he took the glass, sniffed it, and then drank deeply. "Love a whiskey sour. Thanks."

We settled into the rockers on the porch, and within a couple of moments, Santi joined us and picked up his glass from the table where I'd set it. As soon as he was on the swing next to Tom, he said, "So you saw who did this?"

Tom sighed. "I saw the truck. Couldn't get the license plate, I'm afraid. But it was a big silver Dodge 3,500. Bed liner. Marker lights on the cab. Nice truck, but I expect it's a bit dinged up now."

"You saw them ramming the gate?" I asked.

"Heard them first, actually. I was out feeding the boys in the front there and could hear the banging." He took a sip of his drink and smiled. "Sometimes I hear that boy of yours hammering and such, but this was different. Too loud. Sounded like something was wrong."

Santiago nodded. "What did you do?"

"I walked over to the edge of the pasture there." He gestured back over his head toward his house. "And shouted, asked what was going on."

"They heard you?" I asked.

"Nope, but when they kept at it, I hopped on the tractor and came over the bridge. They heard me coming then and took off." He laughed a little. "Guess the hay spike on the front scared them."

I smiled at the image of my seventy-something neighbor in his Farm Bureau ball cap coming to the rescue on his massive Kubota tractor with that huge piece of metal sticking out of the front. It wasn't the most intimidating sight to me, but I guess if you thought that spike might come for your nice truck, it would look different.

"Thank you, Tom," I said. "I don't know what they might have done if they'd gotten to the house." I explained what had happened the night before and worked very hard to keep my voice steady.

Tom pounded his fist into his hand. "If there wasn't a lady present, I'd have some choice names to call whoever is doing this."

Santiago laughed. "Believe me, this lady let several of those names fly herself last night. It was a beautiful sight."

"I bet it was. Well, I'll keep a close eye out for you, and if you want, I have a spare gate I'm not using. Happy to give it to you to replace yours." He finished his drink. "If you'll be here in the morning, sheriff, I'll bring it over and then take the old one to my scrap pile. The guy comes to pick up next week, and he'll be thrilled with the extra metal."

I stared at Tom as he stood. "Wow. Yes, thank you so much, Tom. I really appreciate that." I stood up and gave him a quick hug, under which he stiffened noticeably but didn't pull away.

"It's what neighbors do, Ms. Paisley. I'll lock the gate behind me tonight, for appearances sake," he said as he walked back toward the drive. "See you at first light."

I looked over at Santiago with a smile on my face. "First light, Sheriff?"

Santi's eyes were wide, but I knew he'd be up by then anyway. He was the reason we had the term "morning person."

The evening was lovely with just enough breeze to lift the humidity away, so we sat out on the porch listening to the peepers sing by the stream for a long time. I could feel my fury at the way this safe haven had been violated brewing under the quiet, and I resented mightily the fact that someone had made me have to lock down just a beautiful, open space. But I forced myself to know I was safe, that I was being watched over by both Santi and Tom, and that Sawyer was upstairs sound asleep after he'd had an amazing day. I had much to be grateful for, even as I let my anger work itself through.

Eventually, the mosquitoes got going full-force, and we

retreated inside, where I picked up my tree pattern and Santiago looked through the winter seed catalog to see what he might want to put in his own garden and mine for the next planting.

As I stitched a deep red maple into the fabric, I forced myself to take long breaths and ask silent questions about who would have wanted to stop me from looking into Ethel Orlan's death badly enough that they'd attack my home, twice. I wasn't coming up with any clear answers, but I knew, without a doubt, that these people or this person had made a big mistake by making this about me. They'd brought out my ire, and that man sitting next to me making notes about kale might have looked passive, but he would bring the fury in the morning. As soon as he and Tom hung the new gate that was.

THE NEXT MORNING, Sawyer was still sleeping at five-fifteen, at first light but before the sun came up. I heard Santi slip down the stairs and out into the yard just as Tom's tractor started up next door. For a moment, I thought about suggesting that Sawyer get up to watch, but that would make him interested and he would have tons of questions about the gate that I wasn't sure I was ready answer. Better for him, and for me, to get a bit more sleep.

An hour later, Saw rolled over, put his arm around my neck, and said, "I love you, Mama" before proceeding to tickle me under my chin.

"I love you too, Love Bug. And if you're going to tickle me, I'm going to tickle you." I laughed and grabbed him by the hips, where he was most ticklish, and made him laugh until he asked me to stop.

Then he announced it was time to get up, and we began our morning with a bit more joy than we would have had an hour earlier. That joy was heightened when we came downstairs to find Santiago at the counter with all the makings for blueberry chocolate chip pancakes.

While I took care of Beau, who apparently had not gotten the quality of sleep he'd wanted at Santi's feet and wanted to let me know by yowling loudly the entire time I fed him, the guys made pancakes. Well, they made chocolate-blueberry patties held together with a tiny bit of batter, but they had a blast doing it, so I figured I'd manage to scoop some food into my mouth with a spoon if necessary.

Then, when our food was ready, we all sat down to eat and talk about our day. Santi looked at me and winked. "Sawyer, I saw Farmer Tom from next door this morning. He wanted to know if you and your Boppy wanted to spend the day helping him take care of his cows."

I looked with a tad of concern at my boyfriend, but when he smiled, I decided to just ride along with this plan.

"Your Boppy is going to be here in," Santiago made a point of looking at his watch, "five minutes, and he's excited. What do you think?"

Santi had caught on fast to the fact that Sawyer liked to be able to make his own decisions, and while we both knew that at times, the boy just had to do what we needed him to do, it was nice to see him giving Saw a choice of sorts in this matter.

Sawyer put one finger to his chubby cheek and said, "I'm thinking." Then, he waited a minute, just like I did, and then said yes. As soon as Saw has to think about something, I know it's going to be a yes, which is interesting because when I say I'm thinking it's usually because I'm trying to figure out how to say no.

I smiled. "Great plan. Mind if I come over with you to say hi to Farmer Tom and meet the cows?" I wanted to say thanks to my neighbor, for everything, and I really did love cows.

"Of course," Sawyer said with authority. The boy was confident, and I never wanted that to change. "Let's go."

Santi laughed. "Look at what you and your mama are wearing, Saw-Guy."

Sawyer looked down and then did one of his exaggerated laughs. "I'll go get dressed." Then he sprinted from the table and went upstairs, where I heard a cacophony of opening drawers.

I ate one more spoonful of blueberries and said, "I'd better get dressed, too, and supervise. Last week he came down in his wool sweater and snow boots."

"I've got cleanup," Santi said before giving me a kiss as I headed toward the door.

"Thank you," I said. "For everything."

"You know it's my pleasure," he said as he wrapped up the leftover food and slipped Beau a bite of pancake.

TEN MINUTES LATER, the four of us, with Dad – in his working jeans he'd had for over 10 years and five hundred tears – headed over to Tom's place. The farm was one of the oldest in the area and appeared on a map from 1835. The old farmhouse was tiny, just a couple of rooms on the slope overlooking my house, but Tom and his wife had built a beautiful two-story house just behind it when they'd bought the place fifty years ago. With all the outbuildings and the old fence lines, it was a beautiful farmstead, and the cows just made it all the more idyllic, if you thought piles of poop were idyllic – as I did.

Tom was waiting for us by his run-in barn, and he already had a round bale of hay on his spike. "You guys up for feeding and checking hooves with me?" he said as we walked up.

"Never, ever stand behind a cow," Saw said. "Because they might kick you."

"That's right, Sawyer. I'll show you how to stand beside the cow and check her feet, okay?" He winked at me. "And we'll let your grandfather check on the bulls."

"You can call him Boppy," Sawyer said, and both of the older men chuckled.

"Alright, Boppy," Tom said with exaggeration. "Want to start with the three-day-old calf? I bet they're your favorites."

"You know it," Dad said as Sawyer jumped up and down with excitement.

The three guys waved goodbye as they headed toward the pen behind the barn, where I could see the face of a black calf poking through the slats. It was going to be a great day for all of them, I was sure.

As Santiago and I walked back to my house, I said, "Did Savannah identify the truck?" I knew it wasn't going to be easy since we didn't have a license plate number and everyone and their mother drove big pick-ups around here, but I was still hopeful.

"She's identified all the vehicles that match that description, and she'll be making visits to the owners today." He pulled me close by wrapping an arm around my waist. "We should know who it is by the end of the day," he said.

I let myself relax a little bit. "And while she does that, what are you doing?"

"Well, I still need to go see Terrance Harlow, and I wondered if you wanted to come along. Or if you need to do work, I can drop you at Mika's and ask Savannah to keep an eye on your place."

"If Savannah can keep an eye out here, I'd love to go along." I sighed. "I have work I can do, but the shop isn't scheduled to be open today, and I'm not sure I could concentrate on research. So if you don't mind a ride along..."

"I'll even turn on the lights and siren for you if you want." He kissed me as we reached my house. "You want to shower or anything."

"Is it gross if I say no?" I really didn't feel like the work of showering, and since we hadn't done much the day before, I figured a quick freshen up would serve just fine.

"Of course not – I didn't." He grinned at me. "I'll pack a picnic while you get ready."

I smiled as I went to wash my face and find my baseball cap. How did I get so lucky with this guy?

THE DRIVE to Terrance Harlow's was gorgeous. The bachelor's buttons were blooming in their purple-blue goodness along the side of the roads, and the sweet peas that people planted on the banks around here were all bright in their vine-y pinkness. Even the shimmer of the heat off the pavement made things a little more beautiful, if also serving as a warning to find shade quickly if you don't want to sweat right through your clothes.

Harlow's place was a farmstead at the edge of the town of Rapidan. Back in the day, I expect this road had been the main thoroughfare since so many nice houses – plantations actually – sat along it. But by today's standards, it was just a deep groove in the road barely wide enough for one car to pass through. Once again I was glad I'd bought an all-wheel drive car, just in case.

But we got up Harlow's drive with no problem, and when we crested the hill near his barn, I looked back to a sweeping view of the Rapidan River and the plantations below. This was a prime piece of real estate historically and now. People would pay good money for this view.

When we pulled up, a thin woman in work clothes stepped out of the barn and waved. "Hello. How can I help you?" she asked as I climbed out of the passenger seat.

I smiled. "Is Mr. Harlow around?"

She smiled. "Sure is. He's around—" Her words stopped abruptly as her eyes turned to see Santiago climb out of the driver's seat. "Sheriff." Her voice had turned as sour as a lemon. "Here again?"

"Yes, ma'am. We're sorry to bother you, but we have some new information about the murder. I was hoping Terrance might be able to help us out." He stepped forward and smiled. "Foster Grant sent us."

Something in her shoulders softened, and she let a small smile pass across her face. "Well, then, please follow me." As she led the way around the back of the barn, I studied her small frame. It was lean but strong. Even in her seventies, the muscles in her neck were shaped, and she had the upper arms I'd dreamed of all my life. This was a working farmer, here.

"Terrance," she called to the man bent over a metal water trough. "Sheriff Shifflett is here again. Foster sent him over?"

I could hear the question in her voice, but when Terrance stood, put down the putty knife he'd been using to repair the old trough, and nodded, I saw some of the tension fall from her shoulders.

"Glad you came, Sheriff," the man said as he extended a huge hand. "And who is this wonderful woman?"

Santi turned to me. "This is Paisley Sutton, Mr. Harlow."

When I put out my hand, his large, brown one completely engulfed mine, and I could feel the strength he was holding back from his grip. But he still gave me a firm shake, a shake of respect that knew I could handle solidity. I liked him immediately.

"Shall we all go inside and cool off a bit?" Mrs. Harlow asked.

"That would be lovely," Santi said. "And maybe we could trouble you for some ice water."

"Of course. And maybe a muffin. Terrance just made some fresh this morning." She winked at me. "I do none of the cooking in this house."

"Seems to be a trend," I said with a nod toward Santiago.

"It's a great thing when men know their way around the kitchen."

Mrs. Harlow laughed. "Yes it is, Ms. Sutton. Yes, it is."

"Please call me Paisley," I said as I followed her through a white door at the side of their house.

"Only if you call me Misty," she said.

"Misty it is then." She pointed to a chair, and both of us sat down while Terrance got out plates and napkins and then set a basket of cinnamon-crusted muffins in front of us. Santi asked where the glasses were, made himself at home by filling the glasses with ice and then water before setting them in front of us. "I could get used to this," I said.

"It's a fair distribution of labor around here. We both work hard, but then we can both relax. Right, Hon?" she said.

Terrance grinned. "Not much relaxing on a farm, but when we do it, we do it well." He sat down in the Shaker-style chair across from me, and I marveled at the strength of the chair's construction. It didn't even creak when the huge man sat down. "Please, eat. Like Misty said, they're fresh."

I didn't hesitate and took a muffin straight to my mouth. "It's delicious," I said without even waiting to swallow. "I'll need this recipe . . . for him."

Misty laughed. "I'll write it down for you before you go."

"So Foster sent you," Terrance said as he cut the muffin in front of him in half and gave one part to his wife. "I was hoping word would get back to you. I didn't feel comfortable calling the station, but I definitely wanted to talk with you."

"Everything that comes through the station is confidential," Santiago said. "But you were still worried?"

"What I have to tell you could be compromising for some folks, and while I know you trust your staff, I don't know them from Adam. You'll excuse my caution, I hope." Terrance took a bite of his muffin while he waited for Santiago's response.

Santi nodded. "I understand. I hope it's okay that I brought Paisley."

"Yes, if you want me to wait outside, I can certainly do that," I said behind another mouthful of muffin.

"No, please," Terrance said as he waved a hand in the air. "I only know that in our wonderful, *little* town, word travels fast. So I'd ask that you both try your best to keep us out of the situation if you can. I understand that might not be possible, but I think you'll know why I'd appreciate your best effort when you hear what I have to say."

I glanced at Santiago, who was nodding seriously, and said, "Of course."

Terrance swallowed hard, took a sip of water, and then said, "I was Ethel's beard."

It took me a minute to process all the information that came through in those four words. First, Terrance knew Ms. Orlan's real name. And he had acted as a disguise for her because she was—"Ms. Orlan was gay," I said quietly.

"Yes. She was." He paused there and looked at us. "Misty knew her when they were growing up in Fluvanna. Knew her girlfriend, too."

I looked at his wife. "So you and Ethel were friends as children?"

Misty nodded. "She was friends with my older sister so I knew her well. Susan, her girlfriend, too, all the way through school. That's how she and Terrance met, actually."

Santiago said, "I don't follow."

"Terrance and I met at Jefferson School in Charlottesville and started dating. He'd come down from town every couple of weeks and spend time with me at our house. He met Ethel and Susan there. We were all close, good friends." Misty looked at her husband and smiled.

"When I graduated, I knew I wanted to farm, but the only place I could afford land was up this way, here in Orange. I found this place and bought it with the inheritance my grandfather left me and the money my parents loaned me. It was my dream." He looked down at his hand. "But it meant I had to leave Misty for a while."

"I was only a freshman, and I really wanted to graduate. So we saw each other really infrequently in those couple of years. But we kept in touch through letters, and when Ethel came home from Hampton scared out of her mind, we decided to help her." Misty tugged at her fingers. "Ms. Agee came up with the plan, and Terrance was her contact here."

I sat back against my chair. "So you faked an engagement to the pretend Hortense Agee to double-down on her cover?" I sighed. "Was all that necessary? Was she in that much danger?"

"Susan certainly thought so. She was the one that insisted we tell everyone we were engaged. She thought it would protect Ethel." Misty's voice was soft.

"From her stalker?" Santiago asked.

"Oh, is that what you think? That someone was stalking her?" Terrance said as he shook his head. "Well, yes, but not the way you think. It wasn't that someone wanted to date, Ethel. It's that someone didn't want her to date Susan."

I shook my head. "The person in the shadows at Hampton?"

"Right. That person was following Ethel and Susan around campus when Susan would come to visit. It made both of them terrified, and eventually Susan stopped going to visit. But the person kept looming around Ethel."

"And she was so scared that she withdrew," Santi said.

Both Terrance and Misty nodded. "It was awful," Misty said. "Both women were terrified until Ethel came home. But we all thought they were safe then."

"But they weren't?" I asked.

"He found them," Terrance said.

"How?" I blurted.

"Someone at the school must have told him." Terrance shook his head. "Ethel had been very careful, but she did tell her roommate she was going home."

"And the roommate told someone else." I sighed. "So I see now why you are very cautious about who knows all of this information. It's so easy for something to spread."

Terrance nodded. "When he started coming around Ethel's house, her dad threatened him, told him to get on, but that didn't slow him down. He'd wait at the end of the lane, and any time Ethel went out, he'd follow her. He said that he knew about her and Susan and unless she agreed to marry him, he was going to tell everyone."

"So he did want to date her?" Santi asked.

"Maybe?" Misty put her hands up in the air. "I didn't really think so, though. I think he perceived himself as her savior. If he could get her to marry him, he'd save her from her sinful ways." Misty sucked her teeth and shook her head. "It was pathetic."

"Pathetic but terrifying," Terrance said. "Even to me. We all tried to hide Ethel from him. She stayed with Misty for a while, but when he found her there, she tried living with other friends. He always found her. Small towns . . ."

I nodded. I knew that experience. It was nice to have everyone so close, but not when you needed some space. "So she had to leave. Her home. Her girlfriend. Her friends."

Terrance nodded. "That's when she came up this way. I helped her get settled with my friends the Stones, who I knew through the local Masons. I'd joined up to connect to folks when I moved up here. Humphrey was our Master Mason, and he was a good man. He took Ethel in and despite the flack he got from his wife, he protected her."

"Until her stalker found her again . . ." I sighed. "We know what happened from here, I think." I told them our theory about Mr. Stone preparing a place for her in Lancaster and about how someone had killed her before she got away.

"That's what we think, too," Misty said. "It's like losing her all over again. All this time, we all thought she was safe." She grew very quiet and looked at the tablecloth.

There was, of course, a huge bit of information looming in the air above us, but for some reason, I was nervous about asking it.

Eventually, though, Santiago verbalized what I was thinking. "Who was this man?"

"Allen Marines," Terrance said and held Santi's gaze. "Know him?"

Santiago shook his head, but I said, "Any relation to Bea Marines?"

Misty spun her head toward me. "Her brother. You know Bea?"

I nodded. "Just met her and Enid yesterday." I watched Misty's face and she caught on to what I knew about the two women. "They were lovely. I talked to them because they were students' of Ms. Orlan."

Terrance sighed. "That monster brother of hers has been trying to break them up for his entire life. It's pathetic really."

"But how did he know Ethel before she came here?" Santiago said.

"That the most crazy coincidence in all of this. He was a student at Hampton at the same time she went there. He started stalking her there, but because she never saw his face, she didn't know he had ties to Octonia until after she got here."

I groaned. "Whoa. I mean, I know the world is really quite small, but that seems like a cruel twist of fate."

"Agreed," Misty said. "None of us could believe it when he moved back a few years after college. Things had been so peaceful for so long, but then, there he was. Right at the school one afternoon."

"Tell me about that," Santi said.

Terrance shook his head. "It was a huge fiasco. Mrs. Stone was there, as usual, causing a ruckus about her daughter going to school with 'those people,' and I had come by to see Ethel to keep up appearances but also because Mrs. Stone's ugliness was getting to her."

I leaned forward and watched this big man's face. It was filled with pain.

"When I got there, Allen had her trapped behind her desk. She was terrified, and his face was full of rage. I'm not sure what would have happened if I hadn't gotten there when I did." Terrance ran a hand down his face. "I picked him up by his collar and belt and threw him out of the school. I didn't even think. I just had to get him out of the way."

I fist-pumped. "Good for you," I said. "Did that scare him off?"

"Not even for a minute. I was hugging Ethel, trying to comfort her, when I saw him peering through the window." Terrance sighed. "So I kissed her. She tried to pull back, but I held her lips to mine. It was awful, for both of us, but I wanted to get that man away."

Misty reached over and took her husband's hand and smiled. "She told me that kissing you was like kissing a tree branch. Too rough and scraggly." She put a hand on his cheek. "I like your bark, though."

I grinned. They were so cute. "Did it work? I asked. "Did he leave her alone?"

"He did," Terrance said. "For a couple of days. But then he found out that she knew about Enid and Bea, and that set him off at a whole new level. He started stalking her again, threatening her that if she didn't get out of town, she would regret it."

"We all decided she had to go. She'd get to Lancaster first. Get a teaching job, and when she sent word that she was all established, Susan would follow her up." Misty's voice grew soft.

"But she never sent word?" I asked.

"Susan thought she'd met someone else." Misty sighed. "It broke her heart. She was never with anyone again."

Tears sprung to my eyes. All this hatred and fear had caused so much pain and for no reason other than that people thought some people couldn't love other people. It was ridiculous.

I looked over at Santiago, who squeezed my fingers. Then he asked, "Does Allen Marines, by chance, drive a big silver truck?" he asked.

"He does. Big Dodge. Not sure he's ever put a thing besides a Christmas tree in the bed though. Must be trying to compensate for something," Terrance said with a snicker.

I smiled, but Misty shot her husband a look that silenced his laughter.

"He is horrible," she said, "but he needs love, too." She looked at Santiago. "Why did you ask about his truck?"

"Because last night he rammed it into the gate at Paisley's

house, and I suspect that the night before he's the one who spray painted some hate speech on the side of her home." I could hear the ire in Santi's voice and reached over to take his hand.

Misty and Terrance noticed our grasp and then smiled at each other. "Well, that explains a few questions I had," Misty said. "Glad you two have each other."

Santi grinned. "Me, too." Then, he took a deep breath. "Do you think Allen could have killed Ethel?"

Terrance sighed. "I wouldn't have said so a week ago, but now . . . I just don't know."

"I do. I think he could have, but I don't know that he would have." Misty's voice was firm. "If he got wind that she was leaving town, going far away from here and his sister, he might have just let her go."

"Or maybe, he didn't," I said. "Maybe he didn't want her spreading her 'ways.'" My lip curled in disgust.

"Maybe," Terrance said. "Maybe."

SANTIAGO WAS on the phone to Savannah before I even got the car started. "Start with Allen Marines," he said. "He's our guy, I'm sure."

I couldn't hear Savannah's part of the conversation, but she must have said she was heading over there right then because Santi said, "No, not alone. We'll meet you there. Text me the address."

Out of the corner of my eye, I could see Santiago glaring at his phone, and I reached over to rub his shoulder. "We're getting closer, Santi. We're almost to justice."

He took my hand and kissed it. "Almost isn't there, though, Pais. Sorry to drag you along, but Terrance is right. Word about this will spread quickly, and I don't want Allen to have—"

"You think I'd let you go confront this piece of human scum

without me?" I smiled and pushed down the accelerator. "Don't give me a ticket officer?"

"Turn on the lights," he said.

It hadn't been a regular thing for me to drive Santi's police cruiser, but every once in a while, he'd let me take a turn. Today, it was just about efficiency and safety. He had calls to make and things to put into place, like back-up following us over from Orange County, so it was better if I drove.

I reached down and flipped on the blue and red lights, and then punched the accelerator even harder. I wouldn't bring my son into this situation, but boy was Sawyer going to miss an exciting moment.

ALLEN MARINES LIVED RIGHT at the edge of Octonia proper, not far from Mary's house and our church. His house was neat and tidy with perfectly round bushes out front and a freshly sealed driveway. This man took pride in his home.

It's just too bad he didn't have the same pride for his sister.

We pulled into his driveway at the same moment Savannah stepped from her cruiser on the street. Together, she and Santiago walked up onto the porch and rang the bell. I hung back, on Santiago's instructions, with the camera on my phone rolling. Octonia just wasn't budgeted for on-body cams for its police officers, but Santiago wanted to be sure we had a clear record of what was happening here.

An older man with gray hair opened the door, and when he saw the police, I watched as his expression turned from open to very guarded. I couldn't hear what they were saying, but I saw Marines gesture behind him as if to invite the officers in. Both Savannah and Santiago shook their heads and made a similar gesture toward the small front porch.

Marines reached behind the door, and I saw both officers put their hands on their pistols. But when he came out with a ball cap, they relaxed just a bit and let him step between them and down onto the lawn just a few feet from where I was sitting.

I quietly rolled down the window a couple of inches so I could see if I could catch the conversation on film, but when I did, Marines' eyes darted to the car. "What is she doing here?" he spat. "Why is she filming?"

"She is filming on my request," Santiago said as he stepped between Marines and the car. Now, I was only filming Santi's back, but I was definitely getting the conversation on record. "We need to ask you a few questions about your activities yesterday in the late afternoon."

"I was home, watching television. Why?" He kept trying to look around Santiago to me, but Santi kept stepping into his line of sight.

"Someone with a vehicle matching one registered to you was spotted at a local residence. The truck in question was damaging their property. Do you know anything about that?" Santiago's voice was casual but firm.

"Not a thing. I don't know a thing you're talking about. Must have been someone else hitting that gate." Marine's voice was sharp, but he was still trying to get toward me.

"Who said anything about a gate?" Savannah said. "Sir, I need you to open your garage." She had taken the cuffs off her belt.

"I will do no such thing. This is my private property. You need a warrant to enter." Marines seemed less sure of himself now. His voice was quieter.

"Not with probable cause, sir, and you just shared information about the vandalism that only the perpetrator could have known. You can either open the garage, or we can force it open with a crowbar." Savannah's voice was steady and clear as she stepped toward him with the handcuffs outstretched.

Above Santi's shoulder I could see Marines' shoulders drop

as he said, "Fine." He led the officers toward the garage door, entered a code on the box outside, and watched the door roll up.

Inside, there was the very truck Tom had described, and the front bumper was dinged and scratched. Even from where I sat, I could see the red paint embedded there. *Gotcha*, I thought.

Without another moment's hesitation, Savannah spun the man away from her and put his hands into the cuffs. "Allen Marines, you're under arrest for vandalism and threatening harm." As she walked him toward her car, I could hear her clearly giving him his Miranda rights, and I only stopped recording when she put him in the car.

Then, Santi gestured for me to step out and took my phone to send himself and Savannah the video. "Don't delete this until I say so, okay?" he said as he handed me back the phone. Then, he smiled at me and said, "We got him."

I grinned and smiled back. "No hugs, I guess."

Santiago shook his head. "Don't need to give him any case for thinking he was wronged. But I'll hug you later," he said. "First, we need to gather our evidence. You good to hang in the car a few minutes more?"

I nodded and slid back into the driver's seat. The return trip would be cause for lights in celebration this time.

WHEN WE GOT INTO TOWN, Santiago and Savannah took Marines in to book him, and I walked up the street to Mika's shop. I wanted to catch her up, and I also just needed a little downtime. It had been a busy morning.

I took a detour to the coffee shop and picked the two of us up some lunch and texted Dad to see how he and Sawyer were doing with cow hoof duty. He sent back a picture of Sawyer hugging the baby calf and a note that said, "Good."

That was an impressive message for my dad since I didn't

even know he knew how to take a picture with his phone and typing *Good* on the flip phone required a couple of minutes of effort.

With the boy sorted and three chicken Caesar wraps and three decaf lattes on hand, I headed across the street. I knew it would be a while before I heard from Santiago, especially since the interrogation was going to involve queries about a fifty-year-old murder, and I was glad to have a distraction to keep me busy for the afternoon. Mika was always good to keep my mind occupied in the best way.

Today, though, I didn't need my friends' entertainment to keep me distracted. Her shop was buzzing, and as soon as I walked in, I could tell she needed me more than I needed her. People were browsing throughout the store, and two women were in the front window knitting away. Meanwhile, Mika was teaching a class to a group of home-schooled children, and Mrs. Stephenson was at the register. The place was hopping, and I was thrilled.

I asked a few customers if they needed help, and when everyone seemed to be finding what they needed, I made my way into the back room, giving Mika a pat on the back as I went by, and began pulling out her backstock. Several of the bins up front had been empty or nearly so, and I knew that a well-stocked store made customers more confident about buying.

For the next hour, I refilled crates with yarn, guided customers to the type of skeins they wanted, and straightened the shelves. I even helped Mrs. Stephenson bag up two huge purchases by women who were beginning afghan projects as holiday gifts.

When the crowd finally thinned in the middle of the afternoon, all three of us sat down in the Cozy Corner and took a deep breath. I had distributed the lattes earlier as fuel for the rush, but now it was time to enjoy those wraps that I'd stashed in Mika's mini-fridge in the backroom as soon as I saw it was going to be a while before we could eat.

Now, the three of us put up our feet and savored our good food while we enjoyed the quiet for a moment. "That was quite the rush," I said. "Was that all because of the coupon you put in the paper?"

Mika nodded as she chewed and swallowed. "Mostly. The class came because of our connection to the women up in the Hollow, but the rest was from the ad. We sold a lot, huh?"

"More than I've ever rung up in a couple hours here," Mrs. Stephenson said. "You'll need to get a lot more worsted in if the afghan makers keep shopping. You sold out of five color lots today."

"Thanks for getting the backstock out, Paisley. Am I pretty depleted?" Mika asked.

I visualized the backroom. "You still have a bunch of baby weight skeins and some chunky stuff, but yeah, in terms of the worsted, you're mostly out."

"Whew. I have a shipment coming tomorrow, but I'll have to put in another order for later in the week. The coupon is good through this weekend," she said.

"And this weekend is the County Fair, so you're bound to have more folks who stop in on their way to or from the fairgrounds," Mrs. Stephenson said.

"I had totally forgotten about the fair," I said. "Holy cow. I better get more of my stuff out of storage, too." In recent years, our county fair had stepped up its game from more than just a livestock and pie show. Now, they brought out amusement park rides and musical acts to complement the regular cow judging and squash weighing. It drew a huge crowd and was a big tourist event for Octonia. "Ooh, I have been waiting for the perfect time to put out this collection of ceramic chickens I saved from an abandoned house. Looks like this might be the right occasion."

"You know it," Mrs. Stephenson said. "You might even sell the whole lot to some city girl who wants a 'country' theme for her house."

Mika laughed. "I always love those suburban folks who like to play farm. If only they knew just how much mud the real thing entailed."

We all chuckled at the truth of that and finished our food quietly. Then, I said, "So I helped make an arrest today."

When both women squealed with delight at my exaggerated announcement, I sat forward and told them all about the morning's events, after swearing them to secrecy of course. Both were quite angry with Allen Marines after what he did to my house, but they were glad that he'd been caught.

"So it's probably him who killed the teacher?" Mrs. Stephenson asked.

"Looks likely," I answered. "If he was angry enough to spray paint my house and ram my gate in broad daylight, it doesn't seem a far stretch that he might have killed a woman when he was younger and maybe even more angry."

Mika sighed. "No, no it doesn't. That's so sad." She stood up and stretched. "At least it will give you all some answers, though."

"Yes, and I hope we can give all of Ms. Orlan's students the full story, too. Let them grieve her and honor her, too." I was already thinking through how I might tell her story with respect in my newsletter, and I was eager to see if Rufus and Foster might be willing to let me talk about them, too. I wasn't about to out anyone who didn't want their stories shared, but if they were willing, I'd love to honor their love in that way.

Unfortunately, when Santiago came by about four to pick me up, he didn't have great news. "Marines has an alibi for the weekend we think Orlan was murdered. He was down at Hampton for a reunion. There are even photos of him."

"For both Saturday and Sunday? Because he could have come back, even just overnight," I asked.

"He could have, although he was taking a bus so that would be hard timeline-wise. But he didn't. He was there both days throughout the day, and according to the school archivist, he was very popular that weekend. Apparently, there are photos of him all around campus with lots of different people." He sighed. "I'll corroborate with some of those people, but it's not a high priority since we still haven't found out who killed Ethel Orlan."

Mika sat down hard on one of the chairs by her front window, and Mrs. Stephenson slumped against the other as she said, "So there's still a killer out there somewhere?" She looked out the front window.

"Maybe," Santi said. "Or maybe the killer has died or moved away. It's beginning to feel a bit like we have explored all available avenues to solve this case." I could hear the frustration and defeat in his voice.

I sighed. "Well, let's not give up yet. Maybe we're missing something. Everyone feel like a little late night brainstorming? I can provide cookies, provided Santi and Sawyer don't mind making them while I handle some work emails."

"Sounds like a good plan, but we have to, of course, confirm with the boss when we pick him up." Santi smiled at me.

"If Sawyer is in, I'm in, too, cookies willing," Mrs. Stephenson said. "Maybe the mister could come along. He's so eager to spend time with you folks since I talk about you all the time."

"Absolutely," I said, "and I'll ask Mary, Saul, and Ms. Nicholas to join us, too. We'll make it a party on the porch."

With our evening plans in place, Santiago and I made our way over to Tom's house, where we found him, Sawyer, and my dad all eating popsicles in the shade by the barn. They were each covered head-to-toe in mud, and the look of tired bliss of their three faces lifted my spirits considerably. "Looks like you all have been busy."

"No hoof rot," Sawyer said with a solid nod of his head that I recognized as a mannerism of my dad's.

"Well, that is good news," I said. "Now, would you like to come home and help Santi make cookies?"

Sawyer smiled. "Of course." Then he looked down at his hands. "But maybe I should take a bath first."

All of us laughed, and as Santi strapped Sawyer into the car seat in the back of the cruiser, I quietly invited Tom and Dad with Lucille over about eight.

"Cookies and crime solving?" Tom said. "I'm in."

"Great, and bring your wife. It'll be good to see her." Tom's wife, Emily, was one of those women who was whip smart and so sweet you might have thought she was made of sugar. She wore long skirts and appliqued shirts and sweaters, but I sometimes wondered if that innocent look was a disguise for an undercover CIA agent. She had kicked my tail several times in Trivial Pursuit, and her knowledge of U.S. foreign policy was a bit scary.

"We'll see you then," Tom said. "I'll take a bath, too," he said with a wink as he headed toward the house.

"Me, too," Dad said, "and I'll see what baked goodness Lucille can contribute." He looked at his watch. "I wonder what she can whip up in two hours."

"I am sure we will be amazed," I said as we both climbed into the car for the short trip over the bridge to my house.

WITH SAWYER'S bath complete and cookie baking well under way, I turned to the emails I needed to answer to keep myself from being buried. I made a point of replying to every message I received from my email list. Sometimes that meant five notes and sometimes twenty. Today, I had about twelve to answer, including the ones about the handwriting as well as a few more about Ms. Orlan under her alias as Ms. Agee

These were going to be more tricky than usual since I had to figure out how to be honest and sincere in my few sentences without misleading anyone about the case or giving away too much. I settled on a sort of formulaic response, adjusted for each note, to the effect of, "Your teacher sounds like she was an amazing woman. Thank you for sharing your stories about her with me." It wasn't the most deep response, but it was heartfelt. I had to hope people knew that and would understand my brevity once news about her identity and murder was more widely known.

With those messages handled and the boys still elbow deep in flour, I went to work preparing for the larger-than-expected gathering. When I'd called Mary to invite her, I'd also suggested she reach out to Foster and Rufus and Enid and Bea to see if they wanted to come along. Plus, I gave Terrance and Misty a call, too. Finally, I called Shelley and asked if she'd like to join us. Now we were looking at more than a dozen guests, and my porch just wasn't going to fit us all.

I grabbed my camp chairs from the garage and set up the folding table at the edge of the porch. Then, I got my cardio in by running around the yard to pick up fallen branches for a roaring fire. Finally, I snuck the marshmallows, graham crackers, and chocolate out of the lockbox in the garage where I kept it hidden from my sleuth-like child and set up a display for those who wanted to roast a summer treat.

Between that, hot tea, iced tea, cookies, and whatever Lucille was bringing, we were going to have plenty of sugar and sustenance for a good long conversation. For tonight, I was glad that Sawyer was still sleeping in my room because I could crank the white noise machine and keep him snoozing even if we got a little louder than expected. Although this wasn't exactly the most rowdy bunch, so I expected he'd sleep on.

12

By the time we were done with cookies and then a quick frozen chicken nuggets dinner, Sawyer was basically asleep on his feet. All that time outside in the heat with animals and two grandfathers doting on him had worn him out, and when we topped that off with cookie making, he was basically unconscious as soon as I set his head on the pillow. I stayed with him for a few minutes, though, just savoring his slightly stinky, slightly sweet little boy smell and looking at his incredibly long eyelashes. He was an absolute miracle.

Eventually, I made my way downstairs and found that Dad, Lucille, and Santiago had taken care of setting up everything, including the two key lime pies that Lucille had just whipped up for tonight. They looked absolutely scrumptious, and when I saw her mixing a bowl of fresh whipped cream, I almost groaned in delight.

Outside, the fire was already crackling, and someone had gone into the woods behind the garage and gotten sticks for marshmallows. Santiago came out with pitchers of drinks, and while I grabbed the cooler from the garage and filled it with ice, he and Dad layout the cookies, the whipped cream, with a bowl of ice beneath, and even a cooler of beer that Dad had brought with him. It really was going to be a party.

And to be honest, I needed a party. It had been a hard week, especially with the attacks on my house, and while I was glad to have Marines behind bars and feel a little safer, I was frustrated, too, because we still didn't know what had happened to Ethel Orlan. Until her murder was solved, I was going to be a little edgy.

So a gathering of good people to sort of ground me back in the wonder of this place called home was just about perfect. Add in pie and a little wine, and I was really looking forward to the evening.

As the cars started to arrive just before eight, Lucille met everyone in the drive, explained that Sawyer was asleep upstairs, and directed them around the front of the house toward the fire. I should have expected that folks would come with contributions for the food and drink table, but of course, I had not. Santi went inside and grabbed all my TV tables, and we set up an impromptu secondary staging location with the extra wine from some folks and the macaroons that Terrance had brought over. I was probably going to drop into a food coma when it came time to sleep, but I did not care.

Within a few minutes, everyone had arrived, and we had gathered our chairs around the fire to enjoy the flames and let those who wanted to cook their marshmallows. I was not surprised to see that Ms. Nicholas was able to roast hers to a perfect level of golden-brown without a bit of burning. I had never seen someone so poised in my life. She even ate the gooey goodness without a mess. I needed her to give me lessons.

Santiago and I had talked before everyone arrived, and he'd suggested that it might just be wise to fill everyone there in on all the events of the past two days. We'd keep our sources of information anonymous to respect Terrance and Foster, but at this point, we were at a loss for where to look next. Maybe getting everyone up to speed would give us more leads. At least we hoped so.

So once everyone was settled with a plate of sugar and a cup of something, I announced that we'd recently discovered that Ms. Agee was actually operating under a pseudonym to protect her identity. As that fact sank in, I told them about her stalker and about the threats on her life.

When I detailed how Humphrey Stone and an unnamed man had helped keep Ethel safe, I saw Shelley's eyes dart to Terrance. He gave her a quick nod, but nothing more was said by them or by me. This was Terrance's information to share when and if he wanted to.

By the time I had told them about Allen Marines and the graffiti and damage to my gate, everyone had stopped eating and was just staring at me. I knew the feeling. I'd gotten the information in bits and spurts over the past few days, and everything with my house had turned out okay, better than okay if you counted the new paint job and the new gate. But they were simply flooded with all the data at once. It was no wonder they were a bit stupefied.

When I was done, Santiago sat forward and said, "Now, we need your help. Allen Marines has a solid alibi for the weekend Ms. Orlan was killed, so we still do not know who murdered her. We're hoping that by talking all together we might find something we've overlooked."

"I've found in my work as a historian that oral histories are gathered most effectively in groups because people can bounce ideas off of each other, kind of like you ladies did," I said to Bea and Enid, "with me on Sunday."

"Like pulling one thread loosens another," Foster added. "That makes sense."

"Exactly," I said. "So maybe someone could start by sharing

a story about what they remember about the time before and after Ms. Orlan disappeared. Did anyone notice anything unusual? Any people around who stood out?" I knew it was a long shot to ask for something so specific about an event from so long ago, but memory was a magical thing when it was tugged.

Foster started off. "I wouldn't have really thought much of this at the time. Kids wouldn't, but now, I think maybe she was a bit agitated in those couple of weeks before she disappeared. Do any of ya'll remember how she kept having to look at her notes and sometimes forgot to say our names when we came in?"

"Now that you mention," Enid said, "I do. I even told my mom about it because I thought maybe something was wrong. My mom told me she was probably pregnant." Enid threw back her head and laughed, and I couldn't help but join her.

Given what we now knew about Ethel Orlan, the idea of her being secretly pregnant did seem very funny. Not that it couldn't have happened, of course, but a secret lesbian pregnant and hiding the pregnancy . . . that was the stuff of B-movies.

The laughter seemed to loosen us all up a bit, and soon, everyone who had known Ethel Orlan was putting together a timeline of memory from the weeks before she went missing. Someone recalled that she had left early one afternoon to "get her hair done" but had come back the next day without a new hairdo. Another person said they remember her getting into someone's car one day after school, and they had thought that was weird because she usually just walked to the Stones house.

When I asked if they had recognized the car, no one could remember if they did or not. That probably meant they didn't since their memories probably would have associated the person whose car it was with that afternoon. Still, it was something new to go on.

The conversation bounced around for a while with Ms. Orlan's former students trying to figure out if anyone remembered anything else that was unusual in the weeks before she disappeared. Eventually, though, the threads of memory seemed to disappear, and a rather unsettled silence came over the group.

After a few minutes of letting the fire cracking be the only sound, Saul said, "I have no idea if this might be helpful, but I keep thinking about where we found her body. I mean, whoever killed her had to have been in the school for long enough to get the floorboards up and get her under there before hammering the boards back down." He winced. "Sorry. I know that's a pretty harsh description. But I hope you know what I mean."

Heads around the fire nodded slowly but then Rufus spoke up. "Actually that does remind me of something. I can't be sure it was the same time period that we're speaking of," he said, "but my dad and I were out fishing one evening. We walked back past the school after dark, and there was a light on in the window. Dad thought Ms. Agee, sorry Ms. Orlan, might be in there doing some work, and he went to offer to walk her back to the Stones."

He wrinkled his brow. "When he came back, he said she wasn't in there. That it was just some kid cleaning out the wood stove." Rufus shook his head. "At the time, I thought my dad seemed bothered, but he didn't say anything else. So I just put it out of my head."

"Now, though, you're wondering who the kid was?" Santiago asked.

Rufus nodded. "Definitely. I don't know how I figure that out though."

I stared into the fire for a few minutes. "Who usually took care of the stove? Like who loaded it and who cleaned it out?"

"Usually one of the boys," Bea said. "It was still the days

when women were thought to be incapable of actually doing physical labor."

"Didn't bother me none," Enid added. "I didn't want to get all covered in soot and mess." She smiled, but then continued. "It was usually Marvin who did the cleaning when he was a student, wasn't it?" She looked over at Enid and then to Foster and Rufus.

"Yes, yes it was," Foster said slowly. I thought, for a minute, he might say more, but he just watched the fire quietly.

It felt like we were all waiting for someone to say something else, to fill in more bits of the information that might give us some sense of what was going on, but no one did. And eventually, the fire started to die and people started to leave. Everyone promised to be in touch with Santiago if they thought of anything that might be helpful, and I was glad to have spent the evening with new friends.

But when everyone had left except Mika, Dad, Lucille, Santiago, Mary, and Ms. Nicholas, I said, "Okay, that Marvin Simon tidbit. That's something, isn't it?"

"That cannot be a coincidence given what Foster told us about Marvin the other day," Mary added.

"Sounds like I'll need to go talk to Marvin again," Santiago said. "Don't quite know what I'll say, though. 'So I heard that you cleaned out the woodstove at your school a few decades back? Did you clean it out before or after you put Ms. Orlan's body under the floor?'"

I sighed. "I see what you mean. We don't exactly have a clear connection." I put the last of the dishes in the dishwasher and started it up before walking everyone outside. "Maybe something will come to light that gives us more clarity."

"Let's hope," Ms. Nicholas said. "Let's hope.

. . .

WHEN EVERYONE, except Santiago, had headed home for the night, I plopped down on the couch to try and wind down. It had been a wild couple of days, and my brain was going so fast that I knew that if I tried to sleep now, I'd just lay there tossing and turning. When Santiago said he was going to go to sleep and headed up to Sawyer's bed, I took a deep breath and let myself feel grateful for some time alone.

So I picked up my stitching and turned on the *Rent* soundtrack, which was one of my favorites again, ever since I'd watched *Tick, Tick, Boom!* one weekend while Sawyer was with his dad and Santi was away at a conference. The music made me happy since it was about love and friendship, and after hearing these old friends and new ones laugh and share stories tonight, I really wanted to savor that spirit.

Unfortunately, my savoring was cut short by a text from Foster. "I need to see you and Santiago first thing tomorrow. Your shop. Come alone."

The hairs on the back of my neck stood up, and I felt vaguely uneasy.

Then a second text from Foster. "Sorry, that sounded scary. I just meant that I'd like to tell you what I need to share without anyone else there, if that's okay."

I let out a long breath. "Understood," I said. See you there at nine?"

"Okay," his message said.

I immediately went upstairs to talk to Santi and told him about the text. He had his phone out in a matter of seconds.

I smiled. I knew my boyfriend wasn't a fool, but I was still glad to hear he was going to have back-up coming along. I didn't savor the idea of hearing whatever Foster had to say without some assurances for all our safety.

It was almost eleven, but I still texted Saul to ask if he could have a plan for Sawyer the next day at the lot. His response was quick. "Absolutely. Anything I need to know?"

"Not yet," I replied. "Thanks."

I put the phone back down and looked over at Beauregard, who was squinting at me in disgust since I had disturbed his sleep. "Don't look at me like that," I said. "If I don't get to sleep, you don't either." I leaned over and pushed him off the couch.

His rousing was short-lived since he simply jumped back up and settled into his warm spot again. I, however, was even further from sleep than I'd been before. I grabbed the remote and turned on the TV. *Might as well catch up on Bake Off while I sew*, I thought.

I WOKE the next morning after dreams of filled buns and burning floor boards and found Sawyer still sacked out next to me. It was nearly eight a.m., and when I tiptoed to Sawyer's room, I saw that Santi was still sleeping too. Clearly, we were all tired.

I couldn't bear to wake that little boy, so I slipped downstairs and grabbed a shower before packing a bag with clothes, breakfast, and some snacks for Saw. I knew Saul would, as usual, get him whatever fast food lunch the child requested, so I wasn't worried about that. But he did need to have some sustenance before French fries entered his mouth. Yogurt pouches, string cheese, and grapes would have to do.

At eight-fifteen, when he still showed no signs of stirring, I gently lifted him from the bed and carried him downstairs, where I tucked him in under a blanket and waited for Santi to come down. Saw was still snoring when Santi came down, grabbed a to-go cup of coffee and pulled his cruiser up as close as he could to the house. I toted the boy out to the car and asked Santi to buckle him in before going back for the bags I needed and Beauregard. Even with Marines in jail, I didn't feel comfortable leaving him at home just yet. Besides, if something went wrong with Foster's visit this morning, I figured he might

just rise to the occasion as attack cat. I was hopeful, if unrealis-
tically so.

We didn't talk much on the ride over, mostly because
Sawyer was just waking up and he did not wake well when
disturbed but also because I don't think either of us really
knew what to say. Foster clearly had something he needed to
get off his chest, but the nature of that something was what
had me baffled. Was he going to confess? If so, to what?
Why now?

As Santiago parked, Saul walked over from his office. "I'm
ready for Sawyer duty," he said.

"Thank you, Saul, but be forewarned, the bear has only
begun to stir from his den. He might be a little grumpy." I
leaned into the back of the car and gently lifted my still-floppy
son from his seat. He clung to me for a minute, the warmth of
his sleepy body reaching my bones. "Saw, today you're going to
play with Uncle Saul, okay? Santi and I need to talk to someone
for a while."

Sawyer leaned back, his eyes still partially closed, and said,
"Can I drive the big equipment?" His voice was still quiet with
sleep.

I looked over at Saul, and he said, "Of course. What else
would he do?"

The transformation in that tiny body was almost instanta-
neous. Saw pushed down from my arms and looked up at Saul.
"Let's go," he said, and then almost as afterthought, he shot,
"Bye Mom. Bye Santi," over his shoulder.

" Thank God for big equipment," I said and gave Santiago a
hug. "You ready for this?"

"I have no idea. It depends on what this is," he said.

We walked into the shop, and I took a deep breath. There,
on the middle of the counter was a carafe of coffee and a plate
with two chocolate croissants.

"That man is a saint," I said as I looked at the clock hanging on the wall of the shop. "We still have a couple of minutes before Foster is due. Let's eat."

Santiago smiled. and I turned on the air conditioner. This was not a day when I felt like bearing up under the heat. In fact, if I had to don one of Mika's scarves to stay warm, so be it. I needed to be comfortable for whatever this day brought. As comfortable as possible anyway.

FOSTER ARRIVED a few minutes later and when he stepped out of the car, my heart sank. He looked terrible, like he hadn't slept at all. I really was not looking forward to what he had to say, and clearly, he wasn't looking forward to sharing it.

Santiago stepped forward and shook the man's hand. Foster gave him a single stern nod and then walked into my store and sat down.

A converted shed was an intimate space, and with three grown people sitting in it, three grown people who were definitely a bit edgy, it felt even tinier than usual. But I forced myself to sit still and not fidget. This looked like it was going to be hard enough without me exuding anxiety on Foster.

I offered him a bottle of water, but he shook his head in silence and then took a deep breath. "I know who killed Ms. Agee, um, Ms. Orlan." He didn't look up from his hands, but I could tell just saying those words had taken real effort.

"Okay," Santiago said. "Let's start with something easy. How do you know?"

Foster looked up. "He told me."

I glanced over at Santiago, but his full attention was focused on Foster. "When did he tell you?"

"Last night," Foster said quietly. "After we were at your house, Paisley, I went to his. I already knew what he was going to say, but I needed to be sure. I didn't want to presume, and I certainly didn't want to accuse an innocent man."

"And this person simply confessed?" Santiago asked.

"Fifty years is a long time to carry a weight like this, I suppose. When I asked about her death, he told me. Said he hadn't intended for it to happen, not directly, but now that he'd had a long, long time to think on it, he should have realized how angry he was." Foster looked up at the ceiling. "He's ready to talk to you." He lowered his head and looked at Santiago.

"Where is he now?" Santiago asked.

"In my car." Foster's voice was steadier now that the hard part was done.

I stood up and looked out the window of the shop. Sure enough, I could see the figure of a person in the back seat. I suppose we hadn't noticed before because of the tint on the windows and because we weren't expecting to see anyone else there.

"Would you like to ask him to come in, or should I?" Santi said as he rose from his chair.

"You, please." Foster stood. "If it's all the same, I'd rather not hear the story again. I'll just take a walk if that suits."

Santiago nodded and then followed Foster out the door. I stayed put, not sure what to do in this situation. I wondered if I should go with Foster, maybe stay here as a witness to whatever this man said, take a walk to find Sawyer. My decision was made for me a second later, though, when Marvin Simon walked through the door.

As Santiago pointed to the chair Foster had just vacated, I tried to put together the story for myself, figure out what had happened. But there was just something central I was missing, and I couldn't piece the picture together without hearing what Simon had to say.

I offered him the same bottle of water that Foster had refused, and Simon took it, cracked it open, and took a long hard drink. Then he said, "I killed Ethel Orlan."

"Why?" Santiago asked without rancor.

"If you'd asked me then, I wouldn't have been able to tell you, but I've had some time to think, and the truth is I was scared. Terrified." His voice was small.

"Terrified of what?" I asked, unable to help myself.

"Of being outed. Of being shunned. Of being hurt." He took a deep breath. "Of being myself."

Suddenly, understanding flooded in, and I reached over and took Simon's hand. "You were afraid of being gay."

He nodded. "Even with that man chasing her around like a hound on a deer, Ms. Agee was never afraid. She was strong and clear about who she was, even if she knew it wasn't safe to always show it. She loved her girlfriend and felt no shame for that fact." He took a shuddering breath. "I just couldn't understand that."

I squeezed his fingers but didn't say anymore. His experience was something I could not even begin to understand.

"What happened the day she died?" Santi asked.

Simon took a deep breath. "We were meeting after school, like we did sometimes. The cover was that I needed help with some math for my job, which was actually true, too, but really, we just met to talk. I'd explain what I was thinking about or struggling with, and she'd listen, offer advice if I wanted, but mostly just encourage me to know I was normal, healthy, loving."

I kept holding onto his fingers, and he gripped mine more tightly.

"That afternoon, though, she said that she was going away. That she wasn't safe here anymore and that some folks were helping her move up north and resettle. She told me she loved me, she was proud of me, and that when it was safe, she'd let me know where she was so we could write or maybe I could come visit." He let go of my hand and sat back.

"Something in me snapped." His voice grew very quiet. "The idea that I would be left alone, that she would *leave* me. It was too much, and before I knew it, I had grabbed the poker from the stove and . . . ." Tears streamed down his cheeks. "I didn't mean to do it, but once I had, I knew I had to fix it."

"So you hid her body?" I asked.

"As quickly as I could, I pulled up the boards and slipped her under the floor. I tried to make her as comfortable as possible. I even put her glasses back on." He sighed. "Rufus's dad almost caught me, and I think he suspected something. But when Ms. Agee just disappeared, people didn't know what had happened. Eventually, the questions just faded away."

"For everyone but you." I stood up and leaned over to hug him, but he pushed me away.

"I don't want your sympathy. I've found my way now. I'm fine. I just wanted to be a real man and take responsibility." He stood up. "I'm done talking now. Just arrest me and take me in." He turned around and reached his clasped hands back to Santi. "Cuff me."

Santi looked at me, his eyes wide, but he took out his handcuffs. Then he turned Simon toward him and said, "This way will be fine." Then he slipped the cuffs onto his hands in front of him and led him to Savannah's cruiser outside.

As they drove away, Saul and Sawyer came over. Saul sighed and shook his head when he caught my eye, and I swallowed hard to keep from crying.

"Was that man a bad guy, Mama?" Sawyer asked.

"No, Love Bug. He just did a bad thing because he was hurt. There's no such thing as bad guys." I reached down and gave him the biggest hug he'd allow.

13

Marvin Simon was charged and arraigned for Ethel Orlan's murder. Since he confessed and his attorney didn't protest, there was no trial, which all of us agreed was best for everyone. "Ms. Agee would have not wanted to see Marvin suffer more," Foster said when we all gathered before the sentencing hearing to support Marvin.

"Justice is important, but so is grace," Mary said.

AFTER HIS SENTENCING several weeks later, a judgment that would keep him in prison for the rest of his life, in all likelihood, the mood amongst Ms. Orlan's former students was sober. Although he had been a minor at the time of the crime, he had not come forward for over fifty years. And while most of us probably wanted to go home and just be sad for a while, we had important work to do.

It was the first day of construction on the new Ethel Orlan community center, and Saul and his crew were waiting for us at the site for the official ground-breaking. The newspaper was coming, and even a television station from Charlottesville had plans to cover the event.

When news of Ms. Orlan's murder had eventually spread beyond Octonia, it had been a big story, not just because of her assumed identity and the fact that her body had lain under a building for several decades, but because she was the victim of a hate crime and because she had been killed by a gay man. All of us did our best to play down that last part, especially given Marvin Simon really didn't want to be known as gay. But the media is the media, and soon all of his life story was out there for the world to consume with their coffee. It was very sad.

But the planning for the community center had lifted all our spirits, and I had been honored to be included as a consultant. My role was to help them think about how to use the materials from the original building to honor that structure but also build something that would be usable in the twenty-first century. It had been a fun process, and I was excited to see what was coming.

The plan was to build a large community room from the materials salvaged from the school where people could hold parties or even small wedding receptions. I had already heard talk of a regular Friday night dance there in the hall. I didn't dance much, but I figured maybe it was time to learn.

Then, off the side, near where the smaller classroom had been at Anderson, they were going to install a computer lab, complete with high-speed internet, something our community had been hoping and fighting to get for years. Since the school was on one of the main thoroughfares through Octonia, the county agreed to begin installation of fiber lines there and use the school as a way to explain the slight increase in taxes that their installation would cost.

This room would be open to anyone's use and would triple the number of online computers that were publicly available, lessening the strain on the ones at the library and offering a place for people to take classes on computer literacy, website building, and coding. The buzz about the space was already quite loud.

But it was the outside of the center that was most exciting to me. South of Charlottesville, the community of Porters had put in a public vegetable and flower garden at a former elementary school, and Rufus and Foster had followed their lead and were planning a large community garden outside the building. It would be filled with raised beds that people could reserve in advance, and neighbors would have the opportunity to grow their own food.

Plus, I was going to teach a couple of gardening classes to help people learn how to prepare soil, compost, and tend the plants next spring. That way, the people who used the community plots would be able to tend them well, but also folks who had their own yards could gain a little knowledge. And I was going to have the best co-teachers since Enid and Bea had a massive vegetable garden at their house and were willing to help teach, too.

On ground-breaking day, though, we were simply going to get the soil opened up so that Saul and his crew could get the site ready for construction over the coming weeks. They had bid to do the work at cost, and of course, the community center board, on which Santiago now sat, was more than happy to accept.

So at noon on the day Ethel Orlan's killer and former student was sentenced, we all stood by while Sawyer and Saul used the excavator to begin digging for the foundation. Sawyer was all grins, especially since this special day meant he'd been able to leave preschool early to help with the work.

THAT CHANGE in our personal lives had been monumental for all of us this fall. I missed my boy, and the transition hadn't been easy. But Saw loved his teachers at the preschool in town, and the fact that he now had friends by the dozen gave both of us such joy. Now, he was there four days a week, and I had more space to work and build my business.

Paisley's Architectural Salvage had grown a lot in the past few months. As we geared up for the holiday season, I was able to invest in a second shed/shop, and Saul and his crew helped me open up the walls between the two to connect the buildings. We'd also built a second, larger lean-to on the other side of the new building, so now I had more space for large items.

That was a very good thing because most weeks I had a salvage job to finish, and while I was now pre-selling a lot of the materials I gathered through my website, I still ended up with lots of bits and pieces for the store front. Plus, Mika and I now had our regular booth at the City Market, and with the help of Henrietta, or Hen as she preferred to be called, Claire's best friend, we had plenty of staff to run the shop and the market stall when Mika or I couldn't be there.

Mika's shop was thriving, too, and she had begun offering regular classes to children and adults for a modest fee that really supplemented her income but also allowed others to invest in a hobby without a lot of cost. Her items sold immensely well at both the shop and the market, and she was thinking about expanding her store into her apartment and finding a new place to live.

Santiago's work kept him busy as usual, and the community interest in the death of Ethel Orlan had been all-encompassing for a while, especially since he took it on himself to try and protect Marvin Simon from as much scandal as possible. But once that furor died down, he was back to answering 911 calls from children who were mad at their parents and responding to the scenes of deer collisions. It was a welcome change after such a high-profile case.

And he and I were getting along better than ever. Most

nights, he slept at my house, now in my bed since Sawyer had learned his classmates mostly slept in their own and had learned the feeling of FOMO from his friends. I suspected we might be making things official sooner rather than later, but I was just old-fashioned enough to want him to do the asking . . . at least if he didn't wait too long.

My article about Ethel Orlan and her support for her LGBTQ students, well, it had gotten the mixed response I expected. Some people were furious that I would support such "sinful" nonsense, but most folks were happy to learn that people had been loving people well for decades in our small town. I, for one, was honored to be able to share that story with the names of my friends who had loved each other so long and finally felt safe enough to tell the world about it.

A FREE COZY SET IN SAN FRANCISCO

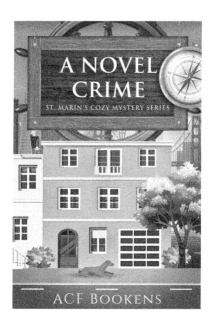

Join my Cozy Up email group for weekly book recs & a FREE copy of *A Novel Crime*, the prequel to the St. Marin's Cozy Mystery Series.
Sign-up here - https://bookens.andilit.com/CozyUp

ABOUT THE AUTHOR

ACF Bookens lives in the Blue Ridge Mountains of Virginia, where the mountain tops remind her that life is a rugged beauty of a beast worthy of our attention. When she's not writing, she enjoys chasing her son around the house with the full awareness she will never catch him, cross-stitching while she binge-watches police procedurals, and reading everything she can get her hands on. Find her at acfbookens.com.

f

ALSO BY ACF BOOKENS

St. Marin's Cozy Mystery Series

Publishable By Death

Entitled To Kill

Bound To Execute

Plotted For Murder

Tome To Tomb

Scripted To Slay

Proof Of Death

Epilogue of An Epitaph

Hardcover Homicide

Stitches In Crime Series

Crossed By Death

Bobbins and Bodies

Hanged By A Thread

Counted Corpse

Stitch X For Murder

Sewn At The Crime

Blood And Backstitches - Coming in March 2022

Fatal Floss - Coming April 2022

Strangled Skein - Coming in May 2022

～

Poe Baxter Books Series

Fatalities And Folios - Coming in July 2022

Butchery And Bindings - Coming in September 2022

Massacre And Margins - Coming in October 2022

65585361R00099